D1456924

UNSEVERED
Bound by Chords of Faith

CHAYA HUDIE MOSKOVITS

First published 2019

Copyright © 2019 by Chaya Hudie Moskovits

All rights reserved

ISBN: 978-1-56871-667-1

No part of this publication may be translated, reproduced, stored in a retrieval system, or transmitted in any form or by any means, electronic, mechanical, photocopying, recording, or otherwise, without the prior permission in writing from the copyright holder and publisher.

Published by

Targum Publishers
Shlomo ben Yosef 131a/1
Jerusalem 9380581
editor@targumpublishers.com

Distributed by
Ktav Publishers & Distributors Inc.
527 Empire Blvd.
Brooklyn, NY 11225-3121
Tel: 718-972-5449, 201-963-9524
Fax: 718-972-6307, 201-963-0102
www.ktav.com

Printed in Israel

ימלא פי תהילתך
Acknowledgments

From the depth of my heart, I thank the Basheffer, our Creator, for enabling me to reach this point and guiding me through every step in the process of producing this book. Without His inspiration, the ideas, words, and perspectives written in this book would not have taken on a life of their own. He is truly the Author of this book and the Author of our individual life stories.

I cannot thank my family enough for their devoted support and praise along the journey. They have invested much effort into this story, and together we have emerged strengthened by its eternal message. My parents instilled in me Torah-true *chinuch* with firm belief that Hashem is the Conductor of our lives, and all that He does is for our best. They spent many hours researching this era to ensure realistic accuracy of details. Their continuous praise and encouragement kept my battery going even when I felt depleted.

My father provided me with the Torah thoughts, translations, *halachah*, and above all *hashkafah*. My mother, a veteran writing teacher, revised and edited every one of my many drafts. She urged me to bring forth layers of depth, like a rose unfurling its petals as it blooms, thus maximizing this saga to its potential. My parents' input imbued me with a pride of being a true *bas Yisroel*.

My sister, to whom this book is dedicated, was my devoted cheering squad during the story's evolution. In addition to unique insights, phrases, and events, she provided the most important thing: a listening ear for every flash of inspiration.

Additionally, I feel indebted to the entire faculty of BYAY (Bais Yakov Adas Yereim Vien) High School in Boro Park, especially Mrs. Kviat, for cultivating an environment immersed in *hashkafah* and *divrei Torah*. Mrs. Weiss, my eleventh and twelfth grade Jewish history teacher, opened my eyes to the Cantonists and their tragic lives. She also graciously assisted me with the research on this topic. I could not have reached this goal during my senior year in high school without my supportive classmates, the graduates of 2018.

I am truly grateful to my editor, Chava Dumas, for her clear guidance and pleasant disposition that made my first publishing experience so smooth.

And thank you to everyone who I may not have mentioned but who provided their input into this book.

Once again, I feel compelled to thank the Creator for granting me this awe-inspiring opportunity to research, write, and show the world the true *emunah* of our People during this tragic era. I cannot thank Hashem enough times for all He has done for me, and all the kindness He continues to do for His children.

Chaya Hudie Moskovits
    5778 / 2018

Dedication

To my dearest Chana Yitty,
You personify the meaning of a true sister.
I could not have done this without you!

Foreword

Dear Friend,

The book you hold in your hand describes the remarkable journey of emunah that my brother, Chaim'ke, traveled upon. Throughout his hardships, he never failed to remember that Hashem, the heilige Basheffer (the holy Creator), is also our Tatte in Himmel, (our Father in Heaven). He knew beyond a shadow of doubt that the Basheffer alone was orchestrating every facet of his life. Chaim'ke possessed an intrinsic belief that Hashem oversees every nuance of life. Indeed, the Basheffer is the ultimate Creator. He places us where we are meant to be. He guides us lovingly. He determines our unique challenges and encourages us to overcome them. The Basheffer constantly gives us strength to follow in His ways, and He expertly prepares our redemption before giving us a nisayon, a challenge.

My brother Chaim'ke was a soldier, but just not any ordinary soldier. True, he was trained to be a loyal soldier for the Czar. But, he stood steadfast in his Torah beliefs and fought faithfully on the front lines in Hashem's Army. In the coming pages, you will find his internal and external struggles that he, along with many other young boys between 1827 and 1857, endured. Although the public knows little of the children who were forced at a young age into the Russian Army, I want to share with you the hidden storehouse of willpower that lay within their tender hearts.

The Russians were intent on eradicating the Yiddishkeit that burned brightly within these children, but this diary proves that the Torah and the Jewish Nation live forever. The Russians could not sully the pure souls of my brother and his comrades. Moreover, the following pages reveal to the world the unsung heroes that must be remembered. With his diary, I feel that Chaim'ke bequeathed me with a holy mission of spreading his brand of faith and strengthening Jews worldwide with the blessed sanctity of Torah-true emunah. The Cantonist Era depicts how precious these Yiddishe children proved to be and how their Torah and sacrifice for Hashem remain priceless.

While riding the waves of Chaim'ke's experiences, you will find many Yiddish words and phrases sprinkled throughout this book. Our main language here in the Jewish enclave of Odessa, Russia, is Yiddish. While translating the diary, I wanted to preserve the purity of my brother's words as much as possible. However, I have provided a glossary of the common Yiddish words used to enable those unfamiliar with our mother tongue to conceptualize the depth of my brother's thoughts and feelings.

This is Chaim'ke's timeless message. Hashem, our Basheffer, is always with us. He puts us in a certain place at a certain time, so that we can fulfill our tafkid, our purpose in life. Hashem holds our hands and leads us through bumps and rough patches as we traverse the road of life with avodas Hashem. He provides us with the inner strength to carry on and remain loyal to His Torah, despite adversity.

My friend, I invite you to read my brother's diary, to get a glimpse of a Cantonist's life. Learn from his everlasting emunah and his fire for Yiddishkeit. And remember that Hashem is with us all the time, that true emunah transcends all.

B'hatzlachah,

Srulik Segal

Prologue

We, the undersigned, promise to stay loyal to Hashem and His Torah. We promise to cling together and help each other stay true to our holy beliefs, despite what may happen to us. We are brothers for as long as we live, and as brothers, we promise to care for each other so that we may be able to live through this nisayon as faithful Yidden. We will join together to preserve and uphold our holy Torah. With due reverence, we sign this pact, binding us forever into a lifelong promise of supportive fraternity.

Shlomo Kofsky
Moishele Kramer
Aharon Baum
Yechiel Abramovitch
Yossel Shneider
Efroym Vassertreiger
Chaim'ke Segal
Cheskel Gordon
Yehuda Levin

1
Thrown Into Turmoil

Odessa, Russia
24 Iyar 5602

I'm so confused. Where am I going? What is happening? What will be with me and my Yiddishkeit?

One thing I do know. I'm with a group of children, traveling in a large, gloomy wagon. I, with many other Yiddishe kinder, are being sent to battle, a spiritual battle.

What do I do? They want to turn us into Cantonists - good Russian soldiers. No one wants to be caught by the Russians! Mamme and Tatte always told us about this. Children have constantly been disappearing from cheder, but only now do I realize that it's scarier than I thought.

I know that everything is from Hashem, but I am so, so scared. What will be? Tatte always warned us to be careful. We tried, we really did, but Hashem had other plans. Today, the chappers came to our neighborhood to fill the quota. When a chapper grabbed me, I fought back, but I was no match for him. He threw me into this dingy wagon with numerous boys my age. I heard that we're being taken to some training camp for Cantonists.

I counted ten children all together. Some boys I know, and some I'll get to know. We'll be together for a while, I assume.

Leibish, my melamed's son, is the oldest. He's fifteen, and he knows more Torah than any of us. He's leading us, encouraging us to stay positive.

"But I don't understand. What's happening?" asked little Yehuda, bewildered and frightened.

He's scarcely eight years old. Who knows how long he'll last under the Russians? Hashem, please have pity on Your small children, and save us from this bitter fate!

"Kinderlach, they're taking us to the big city of St. Petersburg. They will register us as Cantonists and we will be trained as Russian soldiers," replied Leibish, his voice surprisingly steady, as if we are headed to yeshivah and not to an army base.

What's he thinking now? I wonder. The wagon jostled along the dirt roads, narrowly missing the potholes and puddles of mud that were scattered along the road. It jumbled my thoughts into one big mush. I could hardly think straight.

"Soldiers? But we are so young!" gasped Cheskel in astonishment. "I'm only ten and a half!" he added with anguish. "I'll be in the army for practically my whole life!"

I tried to envision our group as soldiers in the Russian army. It would be almost impossible, I realized, to remain a loyal soldier and a loyal Yid at the same time.

The wagon was dark and drafty, casting eerie shadows on our faces. I felt a sudden chill. It was a great contrast to the bright, warm sun that had risen hours earlier. The grayness added to the gloom that we felt, as we realized where we were headed — Gehinnom on earth.

"They train us in a military camp until we turn eighteen. Then, we'll be drafted in the army. But don't worry. We are strong enough to get through this," Leibish reassured us, seeing Cheskel's horror. He smiled wryly.

"I'm not so sure," piped up Yossel skeptically. "I heard that they torture Yiddishe kinder in an effort to baptize them and make them true goyim. I don't know if I can last for so long under torture."

Leibish looked at his bound hands. He had no answer to that. We all knew that what awaited us in the canton was going to be tough. Fear crawled up my spine, gripping me in a chokehold. I feel tied down. My feet are tied, my hands are tied, and the goyim want to tie me to their twisted ideology. How am I going to live through this?

"Why do they want us to be goyim?" queried Moishele timidly. "Why does the Czar care if I am a Yid or not?"

"He wants to convert the Yidden and assimilate them, just like all other reshaim," sighed Aharon. "Leibish, it'll be hard to stay strong if they oppress us. How will we remember to remain Yidden?"

"Don't worry," said Leibish again, pursing his lips in determination. "We have the power to hold onto our Yiddishkeit. Whatever Hashem does is for the best. And if He is taking us to a military lager, He certainly wants us to stay Yiddish, whatever it takes. He gave us this nisayon, and He gives us the koach to withstand it. He won't abandon us."

I know that Leibish is right, but it looked as if he was forcing himself to believe his own words. It's a little hard for me to believe, too. I certainly hope it'll be good. I know that even if it doesn't seem so, whatever happens is for the best. Hashem is with us.

But it will still be very hard to resist. I hope I'll be able to feel Hashem with us, even when we can't see His presence. It'll help me stay steadfast in Yiddishkeit. Who knows what will be with us? We are so, so young. Hashem should help us stay strong.

Chaim'ke Segal
Age 12

2
Chapped!

Odessa, Russia
24 Iyar 5602

The morning dawned bright and early as the sun crept over the port city of Odessa. A bustling city at the Black Sea, Odessa was the center of trade between Russia and the rest of Europe. The air was crisp, and a gentle sea breeze swept among the dusty streets, cooling the warm spring morning. The shops were opening and the people were milling about in the streets, each headed to their own destination. Men and women were on their way to work and boys of all ages were going to school.

It was between Pesach and Shavuos, and the world was in rebirth. Hope for renewal blossomed as the beauty of nature unfurled and grew. Buds were opening, trees were blooming, and the world was bursting with color and life. Spring had rejuvenated the world with its splendor. Peddlers of all kinds were hawking their wares, and young children were running about playfully. Combined with the call of sailors at the dock and the honking of seagulls, a cheerful noise greeted the new day with anticipation.

Two young boys with small cloth caps skipped merrily out of the house during the early morning hours. Black curled *peyos* neatly framed their faces as their sharp blue eyes gleamed into the sun's reflection. They were clothed in handwoven gray vests, with *tzitzis* peeking out, and matching knickers. They were short for their age, and slight of build. Their joy for life was portrayed in the handful of freckles that were sprinkled across their little noses.

"*Leren flaysik*—learn diligently!" their Mamme called after them, pride and love etched in her voice.

Twelve year old Chaim'ke Segal grinned. He and his twin, Srulik, were on their way to the *melamed*, R' Mendel. Tatte, the Rav, had gone to speak with the wealthy community leaders in R' Lazer Gordon's house. He said he had to discuss important matters with them. Tatte seemed concerned, but Chaim'ke wasn't worried. He was sure that the issue would be resolved, whatever it was. After all, Tatte was the master problem solver.

"I wonder why Tatte looked at us so queerly," commented his brother, as they weaved their way through the streets of Odessa.

"When?" replied Chaim'ke, shrugging his shoulders complacently. "I didn't notice."

Kicking some pebbles carelessly, he mused, "But he did seem anxious this morning. I don't know why."

"He was whispering to Mamme before he left, and he was looking at us. It made me feel funny," objected Srulik worriedly. "Did we do something wrong?"

"No," Chaim'ke said, feeling uneasy for a moment. "That is, I hope not."

Their conversation stopped when they approached the *melamed's* house.

"What happened?" asked Chaim'ke, perturbed. "I don't hear anyone in the house. Usually we hear Rebbi learning Torah, even when no one is there. It's oddly quiet."

"Maybe we came too early," suggested Srulik, standing on his tippy toes to peek in the window. The shades were uncharacteristically drawn closed.

"We're a little late, actually," replied Chaim'ke, checking the time on his pocket watch.

"Knock on the door and we'll see what happens," Srulik proposed tentatively, hoping that everything was all right.

Chaim'ke tapped on the door a bit hesitantly. To their surprise, it only opened a crack.

"Run home, boys!" R' Mendel commanded them, tightlipped. "Tell your mother that the *chappers* are in the area. Go hide!"

"Y-yes Rebbi," stuttered Srulik, stunned.

Chaim'ke just stood before his Rebbi in shock. The mere mention of the *chappers* evoked fear in his heart. He was too scared to move. Noticing his brother's fright, Srulik grabbed Chaim'ke's hand, and pulled him down the street. Together, they fled home.

A quota of Jewish boys in every Russian village were recruited to the Czar's army each month. *Chappers* (kidnappers), bribed by the wealthy to keep their sons alone, snatched young orphans and poor children off the streets to fill up the quota. When it was known they were in town, boys of all ages were concealed in attics and cellars. It was dangerous for any boy to be in the streets when the *chappers* were in town. Getting caught by the Russians was the biggest fear the Yidden lived with at that time. They knew that at any given moment, their little boys may just be conscripted to the army, *chalilah.*

"M... mamme!" Srulik shouted as they burst into their home.

Mamme looked up at her sons, alarmed. Why were they home now? They just left for *cheder* ten minutes ago!

"R'-R- ... M-Mendel ... s-s-aid that ... that the *ch-ch-chappers* are coming!" Chaim'ke clutched his chest as he tried to catch his breath. Eyes bulging in fear, he grabbed onto the table edge to steady himself.

"He s-s-said that... that we... we have to h-hide," Srulik added, panic-stricken.

The color drained from Mamme's face and the broom slid from her fingers with a dull thud.

"Boys, come quick!" she instructed nervously, as she ran to uncover the trapdoor that was concealed beneath a chest. She ushered them to the cellar. "Stay here until I tell you to come out. You must remain quiet!"

Scared, the twins scrambled down the drop ladder and huddled close to each other for support. They sat cramped among the sacks of produce and jars of preserves. The air hung heavily, moist and damp. Chaim'ke bit his lip, shutting his eyes in terror. Seeing that his brother was on the verge of tears, Srulik squeezed Chaim'ke's shoulder.

"Don't worry," he whispered tensely.

Chaim'ke looked at him trustingly.

Srulik took a deep breath. His brother was depending on him to stay strong.

"Hashem will protect us," he added solemnly as he tried to encourage himself as well.

From upstairs, they heard baby Perel crying. Nine year old Blima seemed to be attempting to comfort her.

Bang!

A *chapper* stormed in, tearing open the door.

"Where are your sons?" he barked, stamping the mud off his boots onto the freshly swept floor.

"I don't have any," Mamme protested loudly, as she held Blima and Perel close to her.

"I will not leave until I have your sons," he retorted angrily, moving around the sparse furniture in the little house in hopes of finding them.

"But there are none!" she insisted, praying he would leave her alone.

The *chapper* shoved Mamme aside and began ransacking the house, destroying whatever he touched. Perel wailed, and Blima murmured soothingly to her. Seeing no little boys around, the *chapper* swore furiously. Suddenly, he stamped on the floor, eyes narrowing in suspicion.

"It's hollow here. Where are you hiding them?" he screamed, grabbing Mamme by the neck.

"I'm n-n-not..." she stammered, her complexion whiter than a sheet. Fear enveloped her like a thick fog.

Paying no heed to her cries, the *chapper* let go of her and pulled aside a chest to reveal a trapdoor. He yanked it open, cracking the wood at the hinges. Frightened, Srulik scurried behind a large barrel, which concealed him from view. His older twin Chaim'ke didn't budge. He was frozen in shock. He felt as though his feet were cemented in the ground.

"Aha!" cried the *chapper* with glee. "You don't have any boys, do you?" He grabbed Chaim'ke by the shirt collar, cruelty etched in every facial feature.

"You're coming with us," he sneered, roughly pushing Chaim'ke forward.

Chaim'ke, temporarily paralyzed with fright, was unable to react. Dumbfounded, he didn't resist, and out of sheer terror, he forgot who "us" was.

"Chaim'ke, remember that you are a Yid! Don't forget, Chaim'ke!" Mamme called desperately, choking over her words. She burst into tears as she leaned on an overturned chair, her heart heaving like waves in a storm. Other than pray, there was nothing she could do to bring back her son.

"Mamme! Tatte! Mamme!" Chaim'ke shrieked, as he was suddenly hit with reality.

Chaim'ke attempted with all his might to wiggle out of the *chapper's* hands. It was all happening so fast. Feeling his fight or flight adrenaline kick in, he tried valiantly to loosen the *chapper's* grip on him. His mother's cries added fuel to his fighting fire. Chaim'ke kicked and screamed, trying to break free from the *chapper's* iron grasp, but it was too late. He was thrown into a large wagon for the journey to St. Petersburg.

Children were crying, shouting, trying their hardest to resist their attackers. But they were no match for the burly, brawny *chappers*. Every child *chapped* was placed in the wagon that waited in the town square. Their hands and feet were tied to prevent any chance of escape. The entire town crowded around, desperate to save the little innocent children from their bitter fate. The sounds of wailing and pleading were deafening. The *chappers*, however, ignored the distressed pleas of the community and briskly counted the children caught in the wagon. When they realized that there were ten boys inside, enough to fill the quota, the wagon made its rapid exit.

A sudden cloud descended over the city of Odessa, spreading its gloom over the inhabitants.

As he was tossed into the wagon, Chaim'ke looked back to see his mother weeping for the son she had just lost. His mother's last words echoed in his mind. *Chaim'ke, remember that you are a Yid! Don't forget, Chaim'ke!* He was determined to fulfill his mother's last wish.

I couldn't fight the chappers, but I am determined to fight the Russians and remain a Jew. I cannot compromise on my Yiddishkeit, no matter what they do to me! He vowed to himself, as if to compensate for his earlier paralysis.

"*Kinderlach*, we must stick together. Whatever happens, we have to stay *Yiddish*. If we band together, it'll be easier for us to remain strong," encouraged Leibish Rabinovitch, his firm voice hiding his inner fears.

"Are we going to need so much strength?" inquired Yehuda Levin, his voice wavering. "Is it going to be that hard?"

A lone tear rolled down his cheek, but he couldn't wipe it away. The boys' hands were bound with strong rope, locking them in with their bitter future.

"We don't know what will be. Only Hashem knows the future," Leibish answered with conviction, trying to smile at the small boy in an effort to comfort him. "But we have to do what we can to remain loyal to His Torah," he added hesitantly.

With that, the wagon bumped its way along the unpaved roads to St. Petersburg.

3
Forging Ahead

Odessa, Russia
25 Iyar 5602

Srulik apprehensively tapped on the door of his *melamed's* house. Although there was a large Talmud Torah in Odessa, Tatte preferred that his sons learn in one of the smaller *chedarim* of the city. Srulik's Rebbi was Reb Mendel, an old widower but a brilliant *talmid chacham* with a heart of gold. Since no one answered his knocks, Srulik entered his Rebbi's modest home.

In the front room, six boys looked up from their Gemaros in surprise. With a pang, Srulik noticed that his brother wasn't the only one missing. Moishele Kramer and Aharon Baum, who were a little older than him, weren't there either. And where was Leibish, R' Mendel's son? He taught *Chumash* to the younger boys, the five and six year olds. None of the little ones were here today. Was Leibish taken too?

"Srulik!" exclaimed Reb Mendel with a smile, as if the events of the day before hadn't happened and life was normal. "Come join us, we've just started. Did you come by yourself?"

Srulik shook his head. "Tatte came with me," he whispered.

"What's wrong?" asked Mordche Eisen with concern.

Srulik and Chaim'ke loved learning, and it wasn't like them to come late to *cheder*. Suddenly Mordche noticed that his friend came alone.

"Where's Chaim'ke?" Chaim'ke and Srulik were *never* separated.

Srulik shrugged, feeling miserable. He knew that if he began explaining, he'd burst into tears.

"Let's continue," urged Reb Mendel, in an effort to divert the attention from the missing boys. "*Amar Rava tanu rabbanan...*"

Mordche guiltily turned back to his Gemara, and the boys resumed learning the *sugya*. Srulik removed a Gemara from the bookshelf and joined his friends. But he couldn't concentrate. His mind was on his lost brother; yesterday's chaos had traumatized him.

He felt as though he was missing a part of himself. Grief spread web-like around his brain, rendering it numb. It was hard for him to face the bitter reality. Chaim'ke was conscripted to the Czar's army. Srulik was likely to never to see his brother again. He had cried himself to sleep last night, and now, he had yet to calm down. Sadness coursed through his blood freely like fish swimming with the outgoing tide.

Where is Chaim'ke now? He wondered anxiously. *Will I ever see him again? Have I just lost my brother forever? He's being taken to the army. Will he stay strong? Will he remember everything Tatte taught us? Oy, heilige Basheffer, protect him!*

"*Srulik, vos iz de kashe fun di Rashba?* What is the Rashba's question?" a voice broke into his pain. Srulik jumped like a frightened rabbit.

"Umm..." was all he could muster, turning a deep shade of pink.

Deep crease lines etched themselves on the *melamed's* forehead. Srulik was usually the most alert, and now he seemed to be lost in another world. In fact, none of the boys were really concentrating because of yesterday's incident. They didn't know what to make of it. R' Mendel realized painfully that it was his responsibility to reassure the boys, to be *mechazek* them.

"Srulik, are you scared for Chaim'ke?" asked R' Mendel softly. He had heard that the Rav's son was taken just a day before, when the *chappers* had let loose in the streets, hounding for prey.

Srulik nodded mutely, trying bravely to stop the tears that were threatening to flood his eyes.

"Why?" piped up Nissim Weiss.

"B-b-because…" Srulik stuttered. "B-because h-he was t-t-taken to the a-army…"

The distressed boy couldn't hold it in anymore. Srulik's petite frame shook tremulously as he broke down into racking sobs. Reb Mendel put his arm lovingly around Srulik's shoulders. He hugged the weeping boy in an effort to comfort himself and his student. Eyes filled with tears, he addressed the other talmidim with a heavy heart.

"*Kinderlach,* something terrible happened." He stopped to catch his breath, thinking of his own son, Leibish. Who knows where he is now?

"Yesterday, ten *Yiddishe kinderlach* were *chapped* by the Russians for the Czar's army."

The boys stared at their Rebbi in fright.

"We are in *galus,* and Hashem's Face is hidden," R' Mendel continued gently. "We don't know why these things happen. But we believe that the Torah is *emes,*" he continued with a passion, banging his free hand on the table for emphasis. "We have to be strong even when we are hurting inside. We must continue to learn the *heilige* Torah with *hislahavus* and a *bren* as a *z'chus* for them. The *Basheffer* is with them, protecting every *Yiddishe* child from harm."

"S-so w-w-what c-can we do?" asked Srulik, in a shaky voice, rubbing his wet cheeks vigorously.

"The only thing we can do now is *daven* for them," answered R' Mendel tenderly. "The Cantonists need a lot of our *tefillos.* We must never give up hope. We are never alone in our pain. Hashem is with us all the time. Let's say a *perek* of *Tehillim* for them." Reb Mendel paused, seeing the pure faces of his *talmidim* looking up at him trustingly. They began to *daven,* innocent children praying earnestly for the *geulah shelaimah.*

"*Mimama'akim kirasicha Hashem… from the depths I call to You, Hashem…*" the young boys chorused with earnest piety.

Tatte in Himmel, thought R' Mendel pensively. *Please look at your precious kinderlach here, and remember the others who were just taken yesterday. Hear their cries and strengthen them, for we can't be with the ones who were captured, to encourage them. Help them stay steadfast in your Torah, no matter what comes their way!*

4
A Life of Torah

On the way to St. Petersburg
28 Iyar 5602

We stopped in an inn for the night because it started to pour. The officers tried to tug the horses forward, but despite all the curses, they couldn't go further through the thick, molasses-like mud. Resigned to the fact that we couldn't go on, the officers told the innkeeper to stick us somewhere. They untied our hands and feet so that we could walk.

Now, baruch Hashem, my hands are free to write. As we were traveling, I tried to scribble my thoughts in my diary. They bound our hands in the front, and Moishele was kind enough to help me. He held the inkstand I carried in my pocket, and I clumsily wrote the previous entry. That's why it's so messy. I hope I'll be able to read my handwriting and draw chizuk from Leibish's words.

My inkstand and small quill are pure hashgacha pratis. Both were in my pocket, together with my diary, when we were chapped. I now have with what to inscribe our chizuk to strengthen ourselves as we live through this ordeal. Hashem is showing us that He has faith in us and He will guide us through this galus.

We are crammed in a humid, stuffy barn. There is only hay, hay, and some more hay in sight. Well, there is a cow, too. The air is suffocating, and there is no ventilation. The door is locked, of course, so we can't escape, and there is no window. The hay pricks and scratches me all over. The innkeeper gave us a bit of the cow's milk, but we couldn't eat his soup- it had chunks of meat in it. The officers tried to convince us to eat it, but Leibish emboldened us to remain firm.

"The meat is certainly treife. We are holy neshamos," he said resolutely, "and we won't dare bring non-kosher food to our lips."

We barely had what to eat today, and there is a strange empty feeling in my stomach. It may stay there for a while if we refuse to eat treife every day. I know why Leibish is so adamant; it's because we are Yidden. We are special, unlike the gentiles. We have to stay separate from the goyim so we will remain holy children of Hashem. If it's through refusing treife food, then that is what we must do! We are very hungry, but we believe that Hashem will help us through this. He is the only One Who gives us koach, and we place our trust in Him to help us through this journey.

"Let's learn a bit," Leibish suggested when the officers left us to eat their meal and fill themselves up with vodka. "If we review the heilige Torah, we'll be stronger in our emunah during this matzav."

"But Leibish," protested Cheskel, "We don't have Chumashim or Gemaros! How will we learn without the text in front of us?"

"We can learn without them," piped up Aharon. "Leibish knows the Chumash and Gemara by heart."

Leibish reddened in embarrassment. He abhorred being publicly praised.

"From where will we start?" asked Yehuda. "We all learned different things at home. We all went to different chedarim. And I'm much younger than everyone else. I don't know as much as you all do!"

"We'll begin from the beginning, like all little boys do," Leibish replied with a wistful smile. "Bereishis bara Elokim..."

He told us fascinating Midrashim about the Creation of the World. We discussed the purpose of Creation: our tafkid in this world. The time passed quickly as we explored the depth of the heilige Torah and its secrets with our teacher, Leibish.

"We were created to keep the Torah, no matter the circumstances!" Leibish declared fervently. "The reason why we are here today is because the Basheffer wants us to fulfill His Torah at all times!"

We are huddled together for strength and encouragement. If we stay strong as a group, it'll be a bit easier to pull through this as Yidden. It's hard now, and I have a feeling it'll get harder soon. But I know that we aren't alone. Our Tatte in Himmel is here with us, even in this barn. He'll help us stay loyal to His Torah!

Chaim'ke Segal
Age 12

Odessa, Russia
6 Sivan 5602

Although the hour was late, the *Beis Midrash* was alive with the sweet sound of Torah. It was *Shavuos*, the day of *Matan Torah*, and as is the custom, men and boys of all ages were learning the holy Torah all through the night. *Hadassim* and flowers in every corner perfumed the air, adorning the *Beis Midrash* in honor of the Yom Tov.

At one of the front tables sat the Rav of Odessa and his son, delving into the secrets of the *Mishnah* that lay before them. Rav Segal noticed that Srulik kept looking over his father's shoulder, as if expecting his twin Chaim'ke to reappear at Tatte's left.

The Rav sighed. Last year, after all, they had been a complete family, and he had learned with his sons flanking him on both sides. Now, there was only Srulik, at his right. It pained him that it was taking a very long time for his son to believe the truth of his brother.

"Srulik," he murmured into his son's ear, "You know that he isn't here."

Srulik looked up, alarmed. He looked as if he was stung.

"Tatte, I know I mustn't contradict my father, but… but Chaim'ke *is* here!"

Rav Segal gazed at his son. Has Srulik gone mad from grief, *chalilah*? What he just said made no sense!

Realizing that his father didn't believe him, Srulik repeated his statement.

"Chaim'ke *is* here, Tatte!" he said forcefully, his eyes full of fire.

Srulik then pointed to his heart.

"He's in here," he continued softly, his eyes wide with feeling. "Chaim'ke has a place in my heart, and I'll always think of him. And I know that in Chaim'ke's heart there is a place for me, and he'll never forget his brother. The *reshaim* can never separate us, no matter what they may do. We are still connected."

"You're right," Tatte whispered slowly, acknowledging his son's empathy. "Chaim'ke is in every one of our hearts, and he's with us all the time."

Srulik wasn't finished.

"And Tatte," he said with conviction, "I know that Chaim'ke is still connected to the Torah. He will *never* stray from *Yiddishkeit*. He will *always* remain a faithful soldier of Hashem, despite the obstacles he may encounter. He will never forsake his Heavenly Father and his people."

"How are you so sure? We don't know the future," Tatte responded quietly. His son's simple faith amazed him.

"I feel it in my bones," said Srulik with a thread of laughter in his voice. Then he grew serious. "I don't know," he answered truthfully, "but I have a feeling. I've known Chaim'ke all my life, and he is strong enough to win the battle with the Russians, with Hashem's Help. Hashem is with him, and he'll find the willpower somehow to pull through."

"Your *emunah* is unshakeable," admired Tatte, hugging Srulik tightly. "*Chazal* say that one who is wise learns from everyone around them. I can take a lesson from my son's words, too."

"Don't worry, Tatte," Srulik looked up at his father with trusting eyes. "We'll encourage each other in the hard times. We have to stay strong for Mamme and the girls."

"You're right," said Tatte again, this time with a faint smile. "Now that our *bitachon* is fortified, let us continue learning, shall we? We will finish this *Mishnah* as a *z'chus* for Chaim'ke. Hashem will do the rest."

Srulik nodded eagerly, and together, father and son immersed themselves in the sweetness of the Torah, their strong established *emunah* reinforced.

5
Forward March!

On the way to St. Petersburg
10 Sivan 5602

As we stop off in many towns along the way, more little boys join us. Whenever we arrive in a shtetl, we are manacled and kept in the kahal's main building, usually the shul.

"Remember our faith!" the rabbanim remind us, feeling helpless. There is nothing they can do to save us from our fate, other than davening for our Yiddishkeit to remain intact. "Don't forget that you are Yiddishe kinderlach!"

How can we forget? The reshaim will always remind us who we are, as much as they want to assimilate us. We are still heilige Yidden, no matter what they'll do to us. This is what Leibish always tells us, and I am determined to hold onto my faith and remain an ehrliche Yid, despite what obstacles may lay in my path!

They catch more children and chain them together with us. Mothers cry mournfully when we leave each town. Their hearts are bleeding, for what kind of future lies in store for us? It sounds like Tisha B'Av, even though it was just Shavuos. They are so sad, and so are we. What will be with us? No one knows.

Our group is growing, but many boys aren't living through this wretched journey. At the beginning, they would add more wagons as more children joined us. They wanted to take all of us in one shift. But then last week our wagon's axle broke. We can't fix it, and neither can the officers. They think it's our fault that we have one wagon less, so they punished the Odessa group by forcing us to march. The officers soon realized that the other wagons aren't able to go through deep mud without cracking another axle or two. They then ordered that we must all trek through the sludge to St. Petersburg, while they ride the horses in comfort.

The younger boys, I think they are about seven years old, don't stop crying for their Mammes. We can't console them, because we don't know what to say. Who knows if we will ever see our Mammes again? The officers yell at the little ones to keep quiet as we march. I don't think those reshaim were created with feelings.

We are hungry, tired, and altogether weak. When it rains, we are soaked to the bone, and when it's dry, we are sweltering from the heat. A lot of boys are getting sick. I think it's from the combination of the moldy bread the officers give us to eat once a day and exposure to the elements. They cry from fever, hardly able to move. But the heartless officers don't let us stop. We must walk and walk for hours on end.

We've stopped now for the night at another dilapidated inn, but here there is no barn for us. We are to sleep on the open ground, in the mud and dirt. We've done it many times before as we progress on this wretched journey. The officers chained us to the gate of the inn, reminding me of what Mamme told us on Tisha B'Av; how the Yidden were taken into galus in chains. The innkeeper put a guard to make sure none of us escape. We wouldn't even think of it, for where would we run? We are miles away from anything Yiddish, and we don't even know where we are.

But I mustn't complain. Complaining causes one to lose their emunah, and we can't possibly live without our faith in Hashem. There must be a bright side to things. Baruch Hashem, the moon is bright tonight, so I am able to write about our travels. Baruch Hashem it is summer now, and we don't have to trudge through heavy snow drifts (even though the roads are filthy). It feels fresher to sleep outside, where there is a breeze. We aren't sweating in the stuffy inn, because we are outdoors, and summer nights are pleasantly cool. And our hands aren't bound in thick rope, as we were at the beginning of this journey. Thank You, Hashem, for all the good You do for us, the big things, and even small things! Thank You for a little light from the moon and a quiet moment to write down my thoughts. Thank You that the guard fell asleep, and doesn't know what I am doing, because if he did, I would be punished.

Focusing on all of the Basheffer's chasadim will help us stay loyal to Him. He is with us, after all, even in galus. He will help us survive this. If we place our full trust in Him, we will be'ezras Hashem merit to see the geulah, may it come speedily in our days!

Chaim'ke Segal
Age 12

6
A Yid's Uniform

St. Petersburg, Russia
Rosh Chodesh Av 5602

We've arrived at our destination today, and the Russians counted us when they registered us. We are now a group of eighty boys. As we traveled, our group grew and dwindled, as new boys were caught and others died, nebach. So although it seemed as if there are more conscripts, we have only eighty boys. It may sound like a large amount, but it feels like very little. We are only eighty boys, after all, fighting hundreds and thousands of reshaim in the Czar's army who want to destroy us.

We were given clothes to change into—Cantonists' uniforms. They are many sizes too big, "To last you for ten years, at least," one officer said. The only one who fits into his uniform is Leibish, because he's fifteen and tall for his age at five feet and eight inches.

To replace our hittelach, our little Yiddishe caps, we received hard soldiers' hats with gleaming black brims. The jackets we got are a drab navy, made of heavy fabric. They have shiny gold buttons down the front and on the wrists. The collars are high and stiff. Mine bothers my neck. The baggy pants have white piping along the sides, matching the stripe around the crowns of the caps. They are tucked into boots that are large, black, and clumsy. In a way, they personify the officers - burly, cruel, and cold.

The little leather bag we were given is for small items we will need to have on hand. I can keep you in it, with my quill and ink. I just have to make sure to hide you from the cruel officers. If they know that I possess something Yiddish chalilah, they'll whip the daylights out of me. Oy Basheffer! I'd better be as cautious as possible.

I don't feel very comfortable in these clothes. I'm a Yid, but I don't look like one. I'll tuck my payos inside the cap so they won't cut them off. It'll remind me of my Yiddishkeit, even during this dark time.

While we were changing, an officer noticed my tallis katan.

"Remove those strings, Zhid!" he ordered viciously.

I realized that the struggle for Yiddishkeit had just begun, and it may not be over until the end of my army service. If I don't stick up for the Torah now, I don't know if I'll have the power to do so later on.

"No! They're my tzi---" I protested.

"I don't care! You remove them, or I'll kill you!" he cut me off, venom dripping from every word.

Without warning, he roughly tore my tzitzis, and pulled it off me. He then threw it in a pile, where everyone else's clothes were lying.

"We'll burn your rags, so there won't be a trace of Jewishness left!" he said with authority and malice.

But his goyishe mind doesn't understand that nothing can separate our Yiddishkeit from us. We are always Yidden, Hashem's children, no matter what they do to us. That's what Leibish told the others when we were given the uniforms.

Whether I wear my tzitzis or not, I'm a Yid, and I will always remain one, I tried convincing myself. I hope this experience won't chip away at my armor of emunah, chalilah.

Little Yehuda nearly cried that he'll be in the army for so long, but a callous officer slapped him for being moody and childish. Soldiers aren't supposed to have emotions, I presume. My heart goes out to him, the poor boy. It must be harder for him to face the reality, because he's so young and vulnerable. I encouraged him to take heart, for we must stay as connected as we can to our Basheffer.

We're officially soldiers-in-training now, nebach. They're going to take us to a lager, a military camp, in Siberia. There they'll train us to be good Russian soldiers, until we are old enough and ready to be drafted. Rachmana litz'lan!

But we aren't Russian soldiers. We are never going to be. Hashem chose us to be His Army, and we'll only fight for Him. We are full of fierce determination to follow our Basheffer's Will.

Yet the lack of food, the taunts, and the separation from home are threatening to weaken my resolve. The draft age is eighteen, and that's in an awfully long time. I hope to remain steadfast somehow, but I am wary of what may become of my emunah. Srulik was always the stronger one, physically and in spirit. I hope and daven to be able to hold onto Yiddishkeit and to stay a faithful servant of Hashem, despite it all.

Chaim'ke Segal
Age 12

Siberia, Russia
3 Av 5602

We are being sent to a canton, a training school to turn us into Russian soldiers. When they told us where we are headed, we didn't respond. We were numb with distress. It's scary, being sent to a goyishe place where they'll brainwash us to adapt to Russian society.

I know it's all from Hashem, and everything that happens is good, but how will we manage? It'll be tough to keep our Yiddishkeit intact amidst torture and pain. Who knows if we have so much strength to resist? We are so alone now. Who will help us? "Eichah yashva badad?" We are a single sheep amongst many veracious wolves, like Bnei Yisroel is during galus and like Yerushalayim after the Churban. Leibish tried to comfort us, although he seemed just as frightened as we are.

"Our Tatte in Himmel will protect us. He takes care of us, and will help us stay faithful to His Torah," he stated firmly, though his voice shook a little.

That pacified us a bit, but I don't understand. How is he not frantic now? We're supposed to become Russian soldiers! How can he be calm in such a situation? I couldn't fathom his strength.

"Leibish, how are you so composed now?" I finally mustered up the courage to ask.

"Chaim'ke, how was Dovid Hamelech able to sing Tehillim, even when his enemies were pursuing him?" he countered gently.

"Well," I said, thinking aloud. "He put his trust in Hashem, knowing that everything lies in His Hands. Only He can help us. After all, He is the One Who runs the world."

"Nu, Chaim'ke, you have your answer!" replied Leibish, a shadow of a smile tugging at his lips. "Let's follow Dovid Hamelech's lead and sing a nigun."

He started to sing with us Shir Hama'alos - "Esa einay el heharim, meiayin yavo ezri?" From where does my help come? From Hashem, the Creator of the world.

Leibish looked as though we needn't worry, because Hashem is with us, helping us along. I marveled over his placidness at a time like this. We can learn a great lesson from him. Tatte once said that a person will have menuchas hanefesh if he places his full trust in Hashem. This is where Leibish drew his strength from.

I hope we can do the same. I'm not so sure of myself. Unfortunately, I'm afraid the hunger is making me forget some things we've learned at home. I can't comprehend our tafkid in our desperate situation.

However, because he's our leader, Leibish was separated from us after that conversation. When the officers noticed how Leibish was often encouraging us in Yiddish, they took us outside to a rickety wagon, one that seemed flimsier than the one we started out with on our way to St. Petersburg, which was waiting to take us to the canton. They pushed us on, and refused to let him join us.

"You will stay here, Zhid!" growled the burliest one, holding him back in his claw-like grasp.

"But-but… I have to stay with the rest of the children," insisted Leibish, panicking.

This is the first time I've seen him truly terrified. He's not afraid for himself, but afraid for us. He's scared that we'll lose hope and give up our Yiddishkeit, chalilah, without chizuk. I have to make sure this won't happen! I'll try my hardest to fill his place and keep our group strong, be'ezras Hashem.

"They don't need you! You rile them up against the distinguished Russian officers," the officer snapped grimly.

"But… where am I going?" he asked desperately, seeing no way out of his predicament.

"You will be sent to live with a loyal Russian family to make you a proper soldier," the other one informed him coldly.

Leibish trembled visibly, his face fraught with fear. Hesitation and confusion swam in his previously resolute eyes. A loyal Russian family?! Who knows what they'll do to convert him? G-tt zul uphitten!

With that, we were sent off to the lager. Hashem should protect Leibish. Who knows what will be with him? I hope his resolve doesn't weaken, whatever happens. And who knows what will be with us? We need to stay steadfast, even without him. We must survive this as Yidden! I pray that our Tatte in Himmel helps us stay strong.

Chaim'ke Segal
Age 12

7
Tying a Knot

Siberia, Russia
15 Av 5602

We have been journeying for a few uneventful weeks. Baruch Hashem they were uneventful, although we would like Moshiach to come speedily. Understandably, we are not too happy to reach our new destination, but baruch Hashem we are in a wagon. After trekking to St. Petersburg by foot, I don't think we could walk any longer. We now have strength to discuss important things, like mesiras nefesh and emunah. It'll be easier to fight if we come to the battlefield knowing what we are fighting for and how to fight.

Today, we felt we had nothing more to discuss, and we sat in silence until Yehuda whispered fearfully, "It's going to be very hard. Do we have to fight this battle alone? I don't know if I could do it by myself."

"Don't worry," said Moishele in a comforting tone, while resting a hand on the little boy's shoulder. "We are here to help and support each other through this nisayon."

"But..." Yechiel started, his voice quivering. He covered his mouth with his hand to stop himself from finishing his sentence.

"But what?" I asked softly. "What are you afraid of?"

"That... that they'll separate us again," he blurted out. "If... if
they split us up and send us each to a different goy to work for,
I don't know how I'll be strong enough to stay Yiddish until I'm
eighteen!"

Yechiel was right. What if we are separated? What then? Will we
have the strength to encourage ourselves and stay Yiddish? This
was an alarmingly realistic trepidation. I daven that they won't
disperse us among the boorish farmers of Siberia.

"Oh, they won't split us up yet," answered Shlomo with confi-
dence. "They have to test the waters and see if we will stay strong
without our leader, Leibish. It'll be a while until they decide to
move us. That's my opinion."

Unlike the rest of us, Shlomo is brave and unfazed by the dark
cloud that hangs over us, enshrouding us in black uncertainty.
He is a fighter, readying himself for the battle, like a lion about
to hunt its prey.

"I hope you are right," said Aharon dully, fingering the cuff of
his uniform. "Yechiel has a point. I don't know if I could resist
the Russians on my own."

"Why don't we promise, right now, never to leave each other or
abandon our faith," I suggested with a sudden flash of hope and
inspiration. "We will promise to encourage each other and help
each other stay true to the Torah and remain loyal to Hashem.
This way, we can't ever give up. We are bound by a promise to
persevere, hand in hand, and stay Yiddish together, despite it
all."

The others thought it was a wonderful idea. This was a sure way
to quiet our fears of fighting alone. After all, we have each other
to uphold our Yiddishkeit. Thank You, Hashem, for giving us a
strategy to remain faithful to You!

On the inside cover of my diary, I inscribed the promise that Shlomo dictated, and all of us took turns signing our names. Then we grasped each other's hands to form a chain, our eyes shining with happiness and determination. We are united for the common goal: to stay devoted to Hashem and His Torah!

We are now interconnected and we can never break away from each other to convert, chalilah. We are bound by a promise to each other to remain loyal to Hashem. Hashem will give us strength and willpower to keep this promise, no matter what happens. I know He will, because it is His ratzon that we stay true to His Torah, and He will help us fulfill it as best as we can.

Chaim'ke Segal
Age 12

Siberia, Russia
24 Elul 5602

We've come to the canton. It's an imposing, dreary building in the middle of a wasteland. We are going to live on this lager until we're drafted.

As soon as we arrived, we were commanded to bathe to get rid of the lice and vermin on us. They shaved our heads, because we had lice there too. Now that I have no peyos, I don't resemble a Yid at all. I hope we can remember who we are regardless, because if we don't... I don't even want to think what would happen. We can't convert, chalilah! That's the end!

The officers ordered us to work right away. If we slacked off, they whipped us with what suspiciously looked like retzuos tefillin, worn tefillin straps. Hashem Yeracheim! They use holy tefillin to beat our neshamos out of us!

Even though the work was hard, and we know it will get harder, we encouraged each other to stay strong. We won't ever give up our Torah! Torah is our way of life - it tells us how we must act like a Yid. If we are Yidden, we must keep the Torah to best of our ability, so we can be the best Yidden we can be.

"One cannot separate a Yid and the Torah," I told Andrei, the commander, when he demanded that we abandon Yiddishkeit, chalilah. "We will never give up the Torah, for it is who we are! A Yid is bound to the Torah, and it gives us life."

I don't know where my strength erupted from, but I suddenly understood our battle. I must hold the boys firm in our faith and we must never ever give in! We must fight until the end!

"Without the Torah and mitzvos, we are worth nothing!" I declared, in an attempt to convince myself as well. "The Torah makes a Yid! We are Yidden, and we are proud of it! We will never give it up!" The fierce words tumbled out of my soul, draining me of my strength but filling me up with passion nonetheless.

He beat me mercilessly after that, for my insolence. It was frightening, yet it heartened us all. We know with utmost certainty that we have a purpose in life, other than fighting these reshaim when they try to destroy us.

The Torah shows us how to live, and it gives us chiyus to go on. We live for the Torah, because it helps us live. We are only alive if we abide by the Torah! "Eitz chaim he lamachazikim ba" - The Torah is life to those who cleave to it! Baruch Hashem, we have the Torah to guide us in galus, because without it, we'd be lost and forsaken. We must take care to follow in the Torah's ways, as it alone gives life and purpose to a Yid.

Later in the day, Yuri, one of the officers, came to me privately. Realizing I was the leader of the group, he warned me to beware of the cruel Andrei. Not only does he act savagely, he even looks frightening, with a bulldog face and bushy eyebrows. He reminds me a bit of Haman. Chances are he's just as bad. But we must not despair. Our Yiddishkeit is stronger than the reshaim's tactics. We cannot be scared from men of mere flesh and blood (at least, I hope not).

"These reshaim have no power over us. Everything is from Hashem, even this, and I'm sure it is for the best," is the mantra that I keep repeating, to be mechazek myself and the others.

I don't know why, but to me it seems like Yuri is nice, unlike the other officers. It's strange, because the others are so sadistic. Well, the Basheffer is good to us, and He gave us someone here who has a heart. I hope Hashem will perform more chasadim and take us out of here as soon as possible. After all, a miracle can occur any day – "Yeshuas Hashem k'heref ayin – The salvation of Hashem comes in the blink of an eye."

Chaim'ke Segal
Age 12

8
New Year, Old Worries

Odessa, Russia
6 Tishrei 5603

After the Friday night *seudah*, Srulik sat at the table with an open *Chumash*. He was supposed to be *maavir sedra*, as he did every week, but he found himself daydreaming. It was Shabbos Shuvah; the first Shabbos of the New Year. He stared into the Shabbos *licht*, pondering.

Where is Chaim'ke now? It was just Rosh Hashanah. What sort of year awaits him? Is he holding out? Can he stay strong in the lager, *wherever he is? I certainly hope so.*

"Srulik?" Blima interrupted his thoughts. "Why are you just staring? What's wrong?"

Srulik didn't bother explaining; it hurt too much. It was impossible for him to cohesively articulate his worries. He shook his head, as if to clear it of the qualms that lay deep in the recesses of his heart.

"You wouldn't understand," he finally replied, his voice flat. He turned his face away from his sister so she couldn't see his broken spirit.

"But..." she started to argue.

Tatte then entered the front room.

"Blima, why are you still up? It's very late. Please go to sleep," he broke in, noticing that his son wanted to be left alone.

"Yes, Tatte," Blima said sheepishly, turning to go.

After she left the room, Tatte approached his son.

"Srulik, what's bothering you? Is it Chaim'ke?" he asked softly, pain stamped on his face.

Srulik nodded slowly, his eyes downcast, as a small tear rolled down his cheek. He brushed it away roughly with the back of his hand and bit his lip to stop the tide from gaining speed. After all, it's *assur* to cry in Shabbos.

"Tell me," he said gently, wrapping his arm around his son's frail shoulders, as if to protect him from the next wave of pain, "what worries you?"

"Tatte, is Chaim'ke still alive? Is he still strong? Will he remain loyal to *Yiddishkeit*? All these questions eat me up." Srulik looked up at his father, despondent.

"It must be a hard burden to carry around with you all day," Tatte acknowledged, soothingly stroking his son's cheek.

"And all night. It gives me nightmares, wondering about Chaim'ke's fate," Srulik added, his blue eyes mirroring his anguish for his twin. The pain and worry on his face belied his young features. He had grown up too fast in these few months, and his maturity surpassed his twelve-and-a-half years. "Tatte, I can't learn. I can't concentrate. I can't live. It hurts me too much. What should I do?"

"Srulik, you have to leave Chaim'ke up to Hashem," answered Tatte with a sad smile, understanding Srulik's plight all too well. He, too, thought about his Chaim'ke day and night. How many nights had he cried himself to sleep? How many times had he completed *Sefer Tehillim* and learned *Mishnayos* for his lost son's sake? He tried comforting Srulik with what he often told himself when he found that he was drowning in worry.

"Only Hashem knows where your brother is," Tatte continued, heaving a sigh, "and He will surely take care of Chaim'ke, because we certainly can't. Our *tafkid* now is to *daven* for him and to believe that this is for the best. We are in pain, now, but we must remember to always fulfill '*Ma Hashem shoel mimcha*' – what Hashem want us to do in this world. Even though it's so hard, and even though it hurts, we have to remember how Hashem wants us to serve Him. He wants us to believe in His *cheshbonos,* because we can't possibly understand them. '*Hanistaros l'Hashem Elokeinu*'— what is hidden is to Hashem. But we have to follow in His ways and do His *mitzvos,* because that is what He wants us to do."

"But Tatte, why him? Why us? Why did Hashem send Chaim'ke out of all the other boys to the army? Why, Tatte?" Srulik asked in a distressed voice.

"Srulik, '*Shivisi Hashem linegdi samid.*' We must believe that Hashem is with us all the time, even when it seems as though He is *chalilah* against us. Remember, *Shivisi Hashem* even *linegdi.* Why? *Lamah yomru hagoyim.* Only the gentiles ask why things happen. But we Yidden don't. We know that what we see is too limited to understand the Master Plan. Everything has a *cheshbon,* and we believe it with all our hearts. We know it's good, even though we don't have answers. It's hard for me, too, but we have to remind ourselves to hold onto our *emunah.* Everything is planned to perfection."

Tatte's placating words fortified his son, but Srulik was still left with a question.

"What is the reason, Tatte?" he probed further.

"That we don't know," replied his father simply. "The reasons are for Hashem. We just have to believe in Him. We don't need to know why. Our Tatte in *Himmel* takes care of us, and protects us wherever we are. Everything lies in His Hands. We need to trust Hashem, Srulik. It's much easier, knowing Hashem is our Tatte. We have nothing to fear, *tzaddik'l.* Hashem is with us all the time, whatever happens. Don't worry."

"Thank you, Tatte. I... I hope Chaim'ke knows this and remembers all you've taught us."

Srulik buried himself in his father's embrace, willing to draw strength from Tatte himself. Tatte squeezed his son's shoulders consolingly.

"No need to be concerned, Srulik," he whispered in his beloved son's ear, "The *Basheffer* is with him. He is with all of us."

Srulik smiled up at his father amidst stray tears that spilled out of his big blue eyes, and for the first time in a while, he slept calmly that night.

He and his brother were in Hashem's Hands, after all, and there was no reason to be afraid.

Siberia, Russia
11 Tishrei 5603

Yesterday was the holiest day of the year - Yom Kippur. We know because I am keeping track of the days in the back of my diary. Tatte gave me this diary for my tenth birthday. He gave one to Srulik, too. He told us to write down our chiddushim when we learn because we are growing up to be talmidei chachamim. I've decided to use this diary to write down our chizuk, because we aren't learning Torah here, and we have no chiddushim. The ones that I do have in my diary I review constantly, giving me chizuk from the heilige Torah.

When Tatte presented it to us, he helped us write down the calendar for the next ten years. I now, baruch Hashem, have dates from 5600 to 5610! I don't know how long we will be here, but this way, we can figure out the Yomim Tovim of the coming years. In ten years, Hashem will help us keep the Yomim Tovim at the right time. Baruch Hashem, Tatte helped me write a calendar! Hashem sent us the refuah before the makkah! He is so good to us!

According to my calendar, yesterday was Yom Hadin. They roused us earlier than usual this morning to make up for the work we missed yesterday. They tried to convince us to work yesterday, but we wouldn't. When I explained to them why, Andrei slapped my face, and then dragged me to a forest near the lager.

"I'll hang you from that tree if you refuse to work," he threatened, pointing his finger to what seemed to be the tallest tree.

"It's Yom Kippur. I will not desecrate the holiest day of the year," I replied, shaking, even though inside I was feeling strangely calm. I knew that if need be, I'd give up my life for the Basheffer right then, and it would be the right choice to make. My cheek was smarting from the slap, reminding me who I am and what I am here for.

Andrei saw that I wasn't scared of him, so he pushed me back to the barracks and simply resorted to whipping me. He thought my willpower would make me a good soldier, I guess, and he didn't want to kill me. Since the others followed my lead, baruch Hashem, they were also beaten. But my punishment was the worst, because I'm the leader. I suppose I had better get used to this, because for whatever happens, I'll be blamed and punished.

After the beatings, the officers left us alone sprawled on the floor of the barracks. Slowly, we recovered and brushed ourselves off. Bruised but not broken, we helped each other up and we davened whatever we remembered from the Yom Kippur machzor – Kol Nidrei. Unesaneh Tokef. Avinu Malkeinu. Shir Hamaalos. L'Dovid Hashem. Neilah. I thought of Tatte, who davens from the amud on Yom Kippur, and I was pleasantly surprised to see that I remembered most of the nigunim.

We spoke about the importance of the day, inspiring each other to stay steadfast. Shloime, the oldest now at thirteen and a half, elaborated on the Asarah Harugei Malchus — the Ten Matyrs, which we mention in the piyut of Aile Ezkerah during Mussaf. He encouraged us to hold on until the end. Hashem should give me strength to do so.

"Avinu Malkeinu chaneinu v'aneinu ki ain banu ma'asim. Asei imanu tzedakah v'chesed vihosheainu!" Please, Tatte in Himmel, have rachmanus on us here, and save us, even if we aren't worthy of redemption!

Chaim'ke Segal
Age 12

9
Daily Heroism

Siberia, Russia
8 Cheshvan 5603

Early each day, at six o'clock, the officers come to awaken us. Everything is quiet; even the birds (if there are any here) are still asleep. The dawn hours are bitter cold, especially during the Siberian winters. It's freezing here, and the thin coats they gave us at the start of the winter do nothing to protect us from the chill, and it takes up permanent residency in our bones.

But we can't be sleepy, especially so early in the day. We know that the officers won't let us daven, so we devised a system: we will rouse each other about an hour earlier to daven and plead to the Basheffer to take us out of here. Cheskel still has his pocket watch, and he wakes us up at the predestined time for davening. Hashem wants our tefillos, and we desperately need rachamei Shamayim here. We scurry back to our "beds" when we are done. We lie on the hard ground and try to find warmth from the threadbare blankets we were provided.

We pretend to be asleep when Andrei comes. We are given a few minutes to wash and dress, and then we must stand in formation and sing Christian songs. We don't sing, though. Our excuse is that we don't know the hymns, but the officers don't really notice that we are quiet, baruch Hashem. In a group of sixty boys, where the majority converted, it's difficult to determine who isn't singing. Who knows what would happen to us if they did? They notice everything else we do, nevertheless. And many times they punish us for anything that may be remotely Yiddish.

After the morning drill, a dull soldier teaches us the Russian language, math, history, and geography. He drones on and on, not really interested in what he's telling us. Since we are studying a language, we learn how to write. There is plenty of ink here, so once, after classes, I snuck in to the storage room where the supplies are kept to refill my little inkstand. This way I have enough ink to write down our chizuk in you, diary. I hope it isn't considered stealing, because they let us fill up the inkstands they gave whenever we want. They wouldn't notice that ink is missing, would they? I hope not, because if they find out that I'm using their ink for Yiddish, I'll be in such trouble...

In school, we sit in a large semicircle, all sixty of us. There are a couple of barracks on this lager, with ten boys per barrack. Each barrack has its own commander, and ours is Andrei, that rasha. Sergei and Yuri are his second-in-command officers. I think that Andrei is the meanest commander from all of them.

We are trained twice a day, before and after classes, to stand properly and to march perfectly. It hurts to stand so stiff for so long, but woe to the boy who moves without permission or falls down! We are to become little puppets, following orders without question and without thought. At the end of each training session, we are all sore and aching.

But after school we are put to work, hard work. The lucky ones must help the cooks peel potatoes or other vegetables. The rest of us are assigned to clear the forest near the lager, and chop the wood for the fire in practically every room except for ours. Or we have to work in the offices by keeping them impeccably clean and carrying heavy military packages.

The training is strict and demanding. We are ruled with an iron hand, almost like in Mitzrayim. We are not allowed to fail in any assignment. If we do, we are beaten thoroughly. The work is rigorous and harsh. It's only worse with the cruel officers.

Sometimes they just force us to do the most ridiculous things just to make us convert. They would push a bunch of boys into a steaming bathhouse. Those who chose to convert were allowed to leave the intense heat. Those who didn't had to stay there. Steam would inch its way into every part of their bodies until they couldn't handle the torture. They did this to another group in the lager, and most converted, nebach. Those who didn't passed away from sheer suffocation.

When another group was forced to kneel on hot beans on the floor until they converted, all of them gave in and accepted baptism. Those who converted got better accommodations and better treatment. Those of us who didn't are treated worse than dogs, but we can't give up our faith for anything! Baruch Hashem, Andrei didn't force us to do such horrid things. Yet. I think we would all be in the Olam HaEmes by now if he did.

We have a rest hour after lunch, and then we encourage each other and fortify our emunah. We whisper to each other in Yiddish when the officers are not around, or when they don't hear. We cannot forget our mother tongue and the faith of our fathers, especially when things seem so bleak, and especially when those who converted are handled more humanely. We have to hold on, no matter what!

Oy, Basheffer, it's become so, so difficult. The treatment is threatening to bore holes in our fortress of faith. Please help us stay strong! We aren't living for gashmiyus, only for You and Olam Haba. We speak about the parshah, the nissim Hashem does for us, and the kedushah of Klal Yisroel. We have to remember our heritage. Remembering the Torah ensures us that we won't lose our faith and it will give us hope for the future. Hashem should help us carry on.

Chaim'ke Segal
Age 12

10
The Cusp of Adulthood

Odessa, Russia
21 Kislev 5603

I'll be thirteen in a few days, a real bar mitzvah bachur, mused Srulik. The thought of his upcoming *bar mitzvah* was bittersweet.

Tatte had ordered *tefillin* for both of his sons almost a year ago, when they had been a whole family. Both pairs were now waiting on the shelf patiently, anticipating the big day of the twins' bar mitzvah. Only one set of *tefillin* will be used, however. Srulik now gazed at both *tefillin* bags and wondered what was with his twin.

Chaim'ke probably has no tefillin. *I hope he at least remembers about his bar mitzvah.* He sighed, his heart aching with the familiar pain lodged inside. It choked him at times with its viselike grip on his heart.

"Why the long face?" asked Mamme with a smile, fondly gazing at her son. "You're almost grown up, my *bachur.*"

"I was just… thinking," replied Srulik, not wanting to open old wounds. He knew that his mother was heartbroken over one son, and he didn't want to mar her joy over the other one.

This Shabbos, he was to be *oilah* to the Torah, *be'ezras Hashem.* It was the *parshah* of *Mechiras Yosef*— the selling of Yosef. He took a *Chumash* from the shelf to review his *pshetl* with his father and sighed again.

"Tatte," he said quietly, "I think I know what Yaakov Avinu felt like when Yosef was taken from him."

"Tzaddik'l, Hashem has His Ways," Tatte reassured him, under-standing fully what was on Srulik's mind. "Yosef remained a Yid and eventually returned to his father, remember? We can only *daven* that it happens again in our times, and Chaim'ke comes back to us."

Srulik swallowed hard. He hoped Tatte was right, but he was still concerned. What if he *chalilah...* no, he couldn't think of it. Chaim'ke *will* stay strong! He *must!*

"Let's practice your *pshetl* now, shall we?" asked Tatte, pulling Srulik away from his thoughts.

Srulik tried again and again to recite his *pshetl,* but he couldn't seem to remember it. He was too distracted with the apprehension and fear that he had buried in his heart a few months ago. It had been unearthed when he faced the stark reality of the adolescence he was experiencing in stark contrast to his brother. After a while, Tatte stopped and looked at Srulik, deliberating.

"Srulik," he said finally, "you know that you are still in danger of being caught by the *chappers.* Baruch Hashem, you've avoided them for the past few months, but I think it's time to send you out of their reach."

"To go away? And leave you and Mamme here? Tatte! I would never do that!" exclaimed Srulik, surprised.

He felt a web of fear spread over him. To leave Odessa? Where would he go? Was there really any place that he was safe from the Cantonist Decree? And how could he leave his parents alone? He was their only son now, and he felt responsible for their welfare. Who would care for them? Little Blima? He felt much older than he really was. The thought of abandoning his family for personal reasons was worrying.

"Tzaddik'l, there is no other choice," replied Tatte calmly. "You have to leave Odessa to safety. Mamme and I would like to send you to the *yeshivah* in Volozhin. You're old enough to go, and you would learn much more To-rah than you would here in our town. You might be able to forget some of the trauma and start life anew - a new beginning. Becoming bar mitzvah is a time to apply yourself to learning and growing in Torah and *yira'as Shamay-im.* If you are in a *yeshivah,* away from the danger of the Czar's army, then you will be able to learn with a clear head and much diligence."

"But Volozhin? I don't even know where that is!" Srulik protested.

"It's in Lithuania, in the western part of Europe," clarified Tatte, showing Srulik its location on a large atlas. "Although Lithuania is part of Russia, and the Cantonist Decree applies there too, *yeshivah bachurim* are exempt from the draft. If you are enrolled in Yeshivas Volozhin, we can, *be'ezras Hashem*, avoid any danger of the *chappers*. You'll gain two-fold: you can escape the army and learn Torah in the best *yeshivah* of Europe. The *gaon* Rav Chaim Itzkowitz, *ztz"l*, established it, and the boys from there bear the makings of *talmidei chachamim*. You'll only gain from going, with Hashem's help."

"But to go so far? Tatte, when Chaim'ke comes back, he won't know where I am! What will be then?" asked Srulik, horror-stricken at the thought.

"Srulik, when Chaim'ke returns to us, *be'ezras Hashem*, I'll send him to the *yeshivah* to meet you. Don't worry," laughed Tatte, with warmth in his eyes and hope dancing in his heart.

"If you think that it's best for me, I'll go," Srulik conceded, unable to argue with his father. He was a bit relieved, though, to be away from the claws of the Cantonist Decree.

"I'm glad you agree. Remember, Srulik, only good will come out of this," reassured Tatte, hugging his son comfortingly.

Oh, Chaim'ke, if only you can come with me so we can learn together, Srulik thought wistfully. *We would have each other to depend on and to encourage.*

With these thoughts in mind, Srulik left to Yeshivas Volozhin after his bar mitzvah together with his friend, Mordche Eisen. He took along the diary his father had given him three years before.

If I'll be shteiging in Torah, be'ezras Hashem, I'll have chiddushim to write, he reasoned. He felt a pang. *What is Chaim'ke writing in his diary?* He wondered with a deep sigh. *He can't learn Torah in a military lager. I hope he is staying strong in Yiddishkeit, at least. Hashem should protect him.*

Getting hold of himself, he cast away his depressing thoughts and squared his shoulders. He had to learn for two people in *yeshivah*: for himself and for Chaim'ke. After all, who knew when Chaim'ke would have a chance to open a *Gemara* in the near future?

Though it took them a few months, the lads reached the *yeshivah* safely and settled there for the coming years. They learned and grew a lot, in Torah and in *avodah*, under the tutelage of the Rosh Yeshivah, R' Yitzchak Volozhiner, R' Chaim's son.

Srulik was happy to be there, but he often thought of Chaim'ke, yearning and hoping for the day when his brother would return and join him.

Siberia, Russia
2nd day of Chanukah 5603

I'm thirteen today. I'm a bar mitzvah bachur. I am now an adult and obligated in the mitzvos. But what mitzvos can I fulfill here? I don't have tefillin, or tzitzis for that matter. They took everything Jewish away from us. The only thing I have that links me to my faith is you, diary, and the promise we inscribed in you. Tatte isn't here to lay tefillin on me, or to rehearse with me my pshetl. I can't even be oilah to the Torah, for there is none to be found in this forsaken place.

According to my calculations, last week was the parshah of Mechiras Yosef. Like Yosef Hatzaddik, I was torn from my father's home at a young age. And like Yosef Hatzaddik, I must stay strong and remember what my father taught me, despite the challenges that may arise. It's hard, and I'm sure it's hard for Srulik too, not knowing the fate of his brother, physically and spiritually. I hope he isn't worrying too much about me. It's just like him to worry. And I hope he's learning flaysik and growing in Torah if I can't. It hurts me that I can't learn Torah, but I'll be glad if Srulik could.

But I have to stay strong here. I must fight! If not, the others may give up, chalilah, and then what will be? Where will our

Yiddishkeit be? What will we be worth without Yiddishkeit? Our faith is nonnegotiable! But I know that our Tatte in Himmel is with me, even if my physical Tatte isn't. I daven that I can be mechazek His Children and encourage them never to give up.

Please, Tatte in Himmel, stay with us! Help us, for without You, it would be impossible to remain loyal! Don't abandon us! Have rachmanus on your kinderlach here, and take us out of this cursed place! Then we will be able to serve You properly, with tefillin, tzitzis, and a Sefer Torah. I wait and yearn for that moment of redemption, may it come speedily in our days.

(Habachur) Chaim'ke Segal
Age 13

11
Life and Death

Siberia, Russia
18 Teves 5603

Hashem Yishmor! The situation here is just like during the chur-ban! Then, Mamme told us, four hundred Yiddishe kinderlach drowned themselves so that they wouldn't have to work for the goyim in their temples and be forced to transgress the Torah, chalilah. Here too, part of our group gave up their lives al Kiddush Hashem, rather than be baptized by the Russians.

"Did you hear, Chaim'ke?" Shloime asked me this morning, a rare smile lighting up his pinched face, "Yankel, from Grodno, found tefillin in his officer's quarters!"

Tefillin, here!?! We were almost drunk with joy. When was the last time one of us saw a pair of tefillin? Yankel, I knew, was from the barracks next to ours, and he was his group's "Rebbi" holding them strong despite it all. He had it harder, because some of "his" boys converted a while back, nebach.

"Let's ask him if we could use it during rest hour," I suggested, my eyes shining.

The others, even those under bar mitzvah, nodded eagerly. There was something Yiddish here! Thank You, Hashem! You have not forsaken us here! Baruch Hashem, we who are bar mitzvah are meriting to fulfill a mitzvah none of us have ever dreamed of doing! After all, where would one get a pair of tefillin from in this wasteland? Hashem is so good to us! We worked this morning with extra energy, invigorated with the anticipation of performing a precious mitzvah.

Suddenly, we heard a bloodcurdling scream. It was Yankel! We exchanged frightened glances.

"What's happening to him?" whispered Yechiel, physically shaking. His face was pasty gray.

I dropped what I was holding and ran in the direction of the scream. Yankel was hugging something to his chest, escaping his officer, Dimitri. Dimitri was pursuing him with a whip and a string of curses.

"Give that to me, miserable Zhid!" he yelled, trying to catch Yankel.

Dodging, Yankel held the item tighter and fled. The other commanders, realizing what was occurring, encircled him so he had no chance of escape. Desperately, he threw a wild look around him. Seeing that he was trapped, he noticed me behind a tree and tossed the object in my direction. It was the tefillin! I suddenly understood what was happening. I caught it easily, and hid it in my uniform. Breathing heavily from his exploit, Yankel looked up bravely to face his irate commander.

"Where is it?" bellowed Dimitri, shaking Yankel until his teeth chattered. "Where did you throw it?"

He had watched Yankel toss the tefillin out of sight, but I was hiding from the officers a distance away. Dimitri didn't see me, baruch Hashem, and neither did the others.

Yankel pursed his lips shut, squared his shoulders, and gazed fearlessly at his tormentor.

"I won't let you desecrate a holy pair of tefillin!" he declared, undaunted.

"Whip him!" Andrei yelled at Dimitri in a sadistic voice. "Maybe then he'll talk!"

Agreeing, Dimitri whipped Yankel, infusing hate and rage in every stroke of his lash. With a malicious smile, Andrei invited the rest of the boys to view the spectacle. He knew that it hurt us every time we saw a brother tortured.

Yankel was silent throughout the ordeal, but soon he seemed to be near death. In desperation, he asked Dimitri to be baptized. A few other boys from "his" group joined him in his plea, despite my protests in quiet Yiddish. They figured that what Yankel was doing was the right thing to do, and they knew that Yankel would rather die than be baptized. Something was up his sleeve. Dimitri, thrilled with Yankel's plea, called Father Vladek, the Cantonist priest. They took the boys to the river near the lager.

All the officers were there to see their success, and we were forced to stand there too, to be influenced by the boys' decision. When Father Vladek commanded them to wade into the water to be christened, they obeyed, but didn't stop walking until the water submerged them. A few minutes passed, and no one reappeared.

My brothers and I looked at each other uneasily. We knew what that meant. The six boys who were just with us have given up their lives for Hashem. When Father Vladek and the officers realized they were mocked, their anger grew. The priest flew into a fit of rage, and the commanders punished their charges for our brothers' heroism.

"You'll get no meals tomorrow until you agree to be baptized. You cannot die as lowly Jewish worms!" Andrei roared, shaking his fist at us threateningly.

But nothing he could say will change our minds. After what

we just witnessed, we too are ready to die for the Basheffer, just like our brothers. Everything is from Hashem, even this, and it's a message to us. Hashem is telling us to stay strong, no matter what! We are Yidden, a stubborn nation – Am K'shei Oref, and we will never leave the Basheffer. He is our Father, and He will protect us and care for us here.

We are willing to die for our faith. We must thank our Tatte in Himmel for the tenacity He gave us to stay Yidden, even in this desolate lager.

Chaim'ke Segal
Age 13

12
Mamme's Tears

Odessa, Russia
13 Shevat 5603

"Good Shabbos," said Mamme softly, removing her hands from her tear streaked face.

"Mamme," asked two-year-old Perel, "why you cry? Shabbos we happy!"

She was an inquisitive toddler, constantly questioning the actions of her mother.

"*Shayfele*, I'm *davening* for all of my *kinderlach*, so that they grow up to be *ehrliche Yidden*," replied Mamme with a small smile.

"Oh." The little girl absorbed this information for a moment.

"And why so many *lechtelach*?" she queried further, pointing to the illuminated *leichter* of lit candles on the Shabbos table.

Mamme lifted her up and cuddled her baby daughter. "One *lechtelah* for every one of my *kinderlach*," she answered quietly.

Perel stared, uncomprehending.

"Look," Mamme pointed to each candle as she spoke. "One for Tatte, one for Mamme, one for Srulik, one for Chaim'ke-"

"Who is Ch-Chaim'ke?" Perel broke in.

Blima grew pale. She glanced at her mother, scared. How was Mamme supposed to explain the brother that Perel hadn't known?

There was a stretch of silence, as Mamme groped for the proper words to explain the situation.

"He's… he's your brother," Mamme choked out in a whisper. She hugged her young daughter tightly.

"For him I cry the most," she continued, struggling to keep back her tears. "He's lost now."

"Lost?" Perel's big blue eyes opened even wider than usual, as she tried to grasp what her Mamme was telling her.

This is what Chaim'ke looked like whenever he asked a question, which he did quite often, thought Mamme longingly. *If only he would be here, asking one of his questions with his never-ending curiosity.*

"Yes," she replied aloud, her heart broken. "We have to *daven* very hard for him."

She gazed down at the little girl in her arms sadly and thoughtfully. Perel was silent, thinking of what Mamme just said.

Blima drew close to both of them and, patting her mother's back soothingly, she said, "Don't worry so much, Mamme. The *Basheffer* will bring him home soon!"

"Yes," Perel mimicked her sister's announcement, "Chaim'ke come home."

Mamme hugged them both tightly, drawing comfort from her innocent daughters' pure faith in Hashem.

Tatte in Himmel, she prayed, *in the z'chus of the faith of Your little children, bring home my Chaim'ke!*

She pulled out a *sefer Tehillim,* and began whispering the words, sending her hopes and dreams soaring upwards to Hashem and placing her full trust in Him.

Siberia, Russia
13 Shevat (Motzei Shabbos) 5603

I almost gave up today. They wanted to force us to work on Shabbos. They've been trying since we came, but we held strong until now, even when they whipped us. They usually beat me more than the others, for I'm the Rav's son, the unspoken leader. Today, they whipped me with a leather strap until I nearly lost consciousness. The strap tore at my back, and I felt as though I had no flesh left on me anymore. I couldn't take the pain any longer, it hurt so much. I was going to chalilah ask them to baptize me.

But then, I saw dear Mamme. In my mind's eye, she was crying before the Shabbos licht, pleading before Hashem that her children should grow up to be ehrliche Yidden. I couldn't disappoint her. This is what she'd wept for every Shabbos, and I'm sure she is crying now more than before, that I should be strong enough to stay faithful to Yiddishkeit, no matter what. That image held me back from giving in to the Russians. I felt like Yosef Hatzaddik, who won the struggle with the wife of Potiphar when he remembered his father, Yaakov Avinu. Tatte told us about it a very long time ago, when we were in a different world. If only I could be in that world of purity and holiness! But the Basheffer put me here, because I have a mission to complete. I must keep His kinderlach strong in Yiddishkeit, and fortify their hope in the geulah.

It seemed that I fainted, and when I came to, I saw the others crowding around me. Shloime was kneeling beside me, holding a small bowl of water. I suppose he had wet my lips to revive me.

"Geloibt iz di Basheffer (Praised be the Creator)!" he exclaimed in a mix of joy and concern when I opened my eyes and groaned weakly. "I thought that you wouldn't make it, chalilah!"

He spoke for all of them. The others looked at me, terrified that they lost their leader, chalilah. Yehuda's face was whiter than the snow that lay on the ground beside me.

"Of course I made it!" I whispered as firmly as I was able to. I couldn't let him lose hope. "We are stronger than any torture, because we are Yidden! We'll live through this nisayon as Yidden!"

The others smiled, more at ease than they were before. We were going to pull through together be'ezras Hashem, and I wouldn't abandon my brothers. I tried to get up, to show my brothers that I was fine, but I needed Moishele and Aharon to help me walk. I was not as fine as I made myself seem, and I couldn't move on my own.

Still, I mustered up my strength and told the others about Mamme. They were scared when they saw how limp I was, and I knew that if I didn't say anything now, I'd lose them chalilah. Hashem sends me koach to give chizuk to His children, even when I have no energy to speak.

"Think! What does your Mamme want you to look like now? Our Mammes cry for us every Shabbos that we should grow up to be ehrliche Yidden. Shouldn't we try our very best to make them proud?" I asked them, my words coming out in shallow bursts. I struggled to fight my tears and remain strong, as memories of home engulfed me.

"But our Mammes aren't here," said a small voice.

Everyone turned towards the speaker. It was Cheskel.

"They don't know how hard it is for us to stay Yiddish. Especially my Mamme. She's in Himmel, with the Basheffer, for a long time now," he protested sadly, burying his face in his hands so we wouldn't see him cry. He was whispering so softly that I could barely hear him.

I bit my lip. How had I forgotten? Cheskel's mother was nifteres when he was only three. He has no mother.

"Cheskel, you are right. But we say in Tehillim, 'Ki avi v'imi azavuni vaHashem ya'asfeini' - our parents left us, but Hashem gathers us in. They can't help us here. Still, our Tatte in Himmel is with us all the time, even in this lager. He helps us carry on!" I replied with convinction, squeezing his hand to console him.

I hope I didn't hurt his feelings.

It gave us chizuk, knowing that we have a Tatte Who cares for us with immense love.

Chaim'ke Segal
Age 13

13
Fighting for Life!

Siberia, Russia
2 Nissan 5603

They tortured us today, like every day, to convert. I refused, of course, with the other Odessa boys. Our barracks is the only one now that has no baptized Cantonist, b'chasdei Hashem. We are determined to stay Yidden at all times, with the help of the Basheffer.

Those who gave in over the last few days will be converted to-morrow in a ceremony, and then they'll be treated better. They will receive double portions of meat and vegetables each day, while we, who are strong in our faith, are only served one measly bowl of gruel if we beg for it. They have been issued new, clean uniforms, and they get cots to sleep in instead of the hard ground. And of course, Andrei and the others don't beat them. They'll be good Russians, after all.

The privileges that they constantly promise don't tempt me, how-ever. They may be willing to ease my physical weakness, but not at the expense of my faith. I can't let my Yiddishkeit fade away for a bit of food and a bed! I am not convinced at all. They want to weaken me, because they know that I'm the reason why the other Odessa boys resist baptism.

After our resounding refusal to conversion today, Andrei began a brutal whipping. He whipped me until I saw stars, and I asked for a drink of water. He had stripped me of my clothing to beat me, and I was forbidden to drink without his permission. Andrei held a glass of sparkling water in front of me, as Sergei took over the beating.

"You'll only get it if you convert," he jeered, enticingly showing me the drink.

I was desperately thirsty, but I stood strong.

"I won't. I can't," I replied through parched lips, using my last vestige of strength.

I felt the lash on my back again. But I don't care how many times they beat me. I won't give in.

"Then you won't get a drink, or anything else to eat for the next few days," was his cold reply. Has the man no mercy?

But I couldn't sell my Yiddishkeit for a bit of water. I knew that if I am meant to die of dehydration, so be it. I didn't respond, so he spilled out the water at my feet and left. Sergei threw down the lash impatiently, rolled his eyes at me, and left, too. He was growing tired of my obstinacy.

I couldn't bear it anymore, and I collapsed. Yechiel, who had been watching the entire ordeal from nearby, resuscitated me and gave me a drink from his ration of water in his canteen. We get barely enough water to live on, even though there is an endless river nearby. We cannot refill our canteens, nor do anything for that matter, without permission from Andrei.

"Are you really willing to stay dehydrated and lose consciousness for Yiddishkeit?" Yechiel asked in awe, after he helped me redress and I was well enough to talk.

"Yes!" I replied passionately with whatever energy I had left.

"What if you die of thirst, chalilah?" he pointed out anxiously. "Are we obligated to give up our lives for a glass of water?"

"We have to hold on to the Basheffer and stay true to His Torah," I insisted adamantly. "We are His Chosen Nation, and He does so much good for us. We have to do our best to do His Will. If He wants us to die for His sake, then that is what we must do. And we mustn't put our spiritual lives in danger to save our physical lives. There is life beyond this world. You know that we are living for Olam Haba. There is nothing for us here as Yidden. We can't give up the Eternal World for a bit of water here!"

I am determined to make sure that our group stays loyal to Yid-dishkeit at all costs, be'ezras Hashem. We have to stick together, us boys from Odessa. After all, we are the only children that didn't convert. We promised each other to stay strong, but it's getting harder and harder to keep our promise. I feel personally responsi-ble for them, for we are all from the same city where Tatte is Rav. It tears my heart to think of what happened to the other boys. They conceded, nebach, to the officers' demands. I daven that they will change their minds, because we can never give up our Yiddishkeit! We just can't! Hashem should help us stay hopeful here.

Chaim'ke Segal
Age 13

Siberia, Russia
14 Teves 5604

The officers gave us off from school yesterday. It's their holiday, the one on January 6th, and they wanted us to celebrate with them. (I think it's called "Xmas.")

"Children, you will be receiving some fine meat in honor of the holiday," Yuri told us at lunchtime. He always speaks kindly to us, unlike Andrei.

The others were happy that we were getting normal food for once. We haven't tasted meat in a long while. In the beginning, they gave us dry bread and a bit of watered down vegetable soup, and sometimes, if we were lucky, we got a little gruel. Now, all we have is the bread, almost too hard to chew.

I commiserate with them, because I, too, am starving for normal food. We are growing boys, and Mamme always said that children need much nourishment to stay healthy. Nevertheless, I forced myself to tell them that there was no way that we were allowed to eat the meat.

"Why can't we?" asked Yehuda, bewildered.

"What do you mean?" I countered with a sigh. "They don't want to be nice. They just want us to give up our Yiddishkeit. This meat is treife; we can't eat it."

"But Chaim'ke, we're so weak. I'm sure that now we are allowed to eat it. At this point, it is pikuach nefesh," Moishele protested.

I glanced at my friends, my brothers. It seemed as though he was right. I saw pale, gaunt boys with sunken cheeks and large uniforms hanging limply on their bony frames. I know I look similar, if not more skeletal. We are so emaciated from the torture, that we wouldn't be recognized as the same boys who arrived here a little more than a year ago. If we don't eat now, we may starve to death, chalilah.

"In a time of shmad, there is no such thing as pikuach nefesh!" I told them fervently, despite our great hunger. "We must give up everything for Yiddishkeit, even our lives! Kinderlach, do you want to chalilah lose your z'chusim for a little meat? It isn't worth it! Stay strong! We can get through this nisayon, if only we are steadfast. We mustn't give up now. We've come so far!" A fire for Yiddishkeit was alight in my soul. We couldn't possibly give up!

Chasdei Hashem, we were spared from putting treife food in our mouths. When Yuri came with the plate of meat, he tripped and accidently dropped it face down on the floor. He gave us some bread to eat instead. (I don't know, but I have a feeling that he did it on purpose. I guess he assumed we would refuse to eat it anyway.) Hashem saved us from being forced to eat treife food! He is so good to us! I hope we will be able to recognize His many other chasadim, for it gets harder every day. It's comforting when we feel the warmth of the Basheffer's love for us, even in this cold place.

Chaim'ke Segal
Age 14

14
The Right Choice

Siberia, Russia
5 Adar 5604

Tatte always told us that when we enter Adar, we increase the simchah. I don't know. It doesn't seem very happy now. In fact, it's never really cheerful in the lager, especially now, since we lost one of our brothers.

Andrei loves singling out one of us to torture each Shabbos. This time, he chose Yechiel. He's three months older than me. One of the older ones is always chosen for torture, I guess because we set an example for the others. Andrei beat him again and again, hoping that he'd give in. Yechiel heroically refused to bow to the cruel sergeant's demands.

After a while, Andrei became furious. He threw Yechiel to the ground and set his wild dog on the boy. Andrei always warned that he'd do it to one of us, but I didn't think he'd carry through with his threats. The dog attacked Yechiel all over, and Andrei just laughed cruelly. He forced us to stand there and watch. It was heart wrenching. Yechiel was screaming from anguish, the dog mauling his uniform and body. And the rasha didn't let us help Yechiel and save him from the torment and suffering.

Finally, Andrei lost interest and Yechiel stopped shrieking. Andrei left, taking the dog with him. As soon as he was gone, we ran to Yechiel, who was lying in a pool of blood, motionless. Shloime tried lifting him up, but Yechiel had no strength even to raise his head. He had lost a lot of blood during the ordeal. He gestured weakly to Shloime to leave him alone. Aharon went to get water, in an attempt to clear his face from blood. There wasn't much else we could do. It was Shabbos, after all. Yechiel stirred and mumbled something unintelligible. I leaned closer to hear him.

"Ch-Ch-Chaim'ke..."

"Yes?" I replied anxiously. "Are you alright? Let me help you up."

"N-n-no..." Yechiel tried to catch his breath. He wheezed and coughed up blood. The red of his blood colored the pristine snow that was near him. It scared me. "I...S-say Sh-shema with... me..."

I did. With his last breath, we said the Shema, the declaration of faith of every Yid. Then, with a smile on his serene face, he was gone. He stopped breathing. Moishele checked. We looked at each other, pale and trembling.

"We h-have to bring him to k-kever Yisroel," said Cheskel, his voice unsteady.

Yehuda suddenly burst into tears. He had been controlling himself until then because he knew he'd be punished for crying in front of Andrei.

"Oy, Yehuda'le," I hugged the little boy, crying along with him.

Even though it was Shabbos, we all wept bitterly. We've lost a brother. It's as if we are missing a part of ourselves. I tried to think of what to say.

"Yechiel is in a better place now. He's with the Basheffer, in Himmel."

"I know, Chaim'ke," he sobbed, "But will this happen to all of us? Andrei might decide to do this every day. I know we mustn't ever transgress Shabbos, but if we don't listen to cruel Andrei, maybe he'll set his dogs on the rest of us!"

I was at a loss for words. What should I tell him? Who knows what that rasha may plan to do?

"Believe in Hashem," I said finally, biting my lip to stem the flow of tears. "Hashem is with us, and He will surely protect us."

"But He didn't protect Yechiel," retorted Yossel, stamping his foot in protest.

I looked up searchingly toward the darkening sky.

"Hashem," I prayed silently, "please help me stay strong to empower my dear brothers in Your faith!"

"This is what Hashem wanted to happen," I insisted aloud, trying to strengthen myself, too.

I saw that I was nearly losing them. The death of our brother discouraged us, and if one boy would decide to give up, chalilah, what will be? That can't ever happen to us! We must stay Yiddish, and we must stay together.

"Whatever Hashem does is for the best, even when it seems to be quite the opposite," I told them softly, placing my hand firmly on Yossel's shoulder. "Hashem runs the world. He knows what is good for us, and He helps us take part in His Master Plan. We must believe that with our full hearts, even if we don't understand it."

"Chaim'ke, your emunah is rock-solid," said Cheskel, sniffling miserably. "But some of us aren't that strong. What will be with us?"

"I want you to believe and trust in Hashem just as firmly as I do!" I maintained soothingly, drying his tears, and mine too.

"The only way we can stay Yiddish here is if we believe fully in the Basheffer."

As soon as we saw three stars, we dug a grave behind the barracks and buried Yechiel there. I put up a little marker with his name penned on it, so we know where he's buried. Baruch Hashem, he merited kevurah by Yidden, even though it wasn't according to halachah. We don't know the halachah.

Afterward, we just cried in mourning. At least, we tried not to, but we couldn't help it. My heart hurt. It was painful to see how Yechiel gave up his life for the Basheffer. This is what the talmidim of R' Akiva must have felt like, I realized, seeing their Rebbi dying for the sake of Hashem in the most excruciating way. But R' Akiva was happy, and so was Yechiel. Both were able to serve Hashem in the best way, by giving their souls to Hashem as a korban.

"Although it is ideal that we live al Kiddush Hashem," I related to the others after thinking for a long while, "here, in this lager, we must die for Hashem. Like R' Akiva, we have only one choice, to give up our lives for the Basheffer. We may not be able to serve Hashem with our full capacity, by doing all the mitzvos, but we can serve Him with our hearts and souls. We can persevere for His sake here, and whatever Hashem decrees, whether we live or die, will happen."

"And it'll be for the best, even if we don't understand it," added Shloime softly, "for everything Hashem does is good."

"We must show our fierce love for the Basheffer," I continued, "by sacrificing our physical comforts for Him. There is no way we can live like a Yid here, but there is also no way we can give up our Yiddishkeit and live like a goy, chalilah. We have to take Yechiel's lead and be ready to die al Kiddush Hashem. We aren't on the level of R' Akiva, but I believe that the deed is just as great."

The others agreed with me. We are ready and willing to do the ratzon of our Basheffer, be it through life or through death!

(Baruch Hashem, we are stronger in our faith from this sad experience. I was afraid of the opposite. To be honest, I felt myself wavering a bit after saying Shema with Yechiel, Hy"d.)

Chaim'ke Segal
Age 14

15
The Tree of Life

Volozhin, Russia
5 Adar 5604
To my dear Tatte,
I hope all is well at home. Baruch Hashem, I am learning very well.
We learn a lot here in yeshivah. The Rosh Yeshivah insists that there
is always someone learning in yeshivah, no matter the hour. He quotes
his saintly father, Rav Chaim, who says that the world stands only on
learning Torah. Torah must be learned all the time, so that the world's
existence is maintained, that it has a kiyum.
My greatest desire is to know all of Shas. The Rosh Yeshivah wants
us to know as much as we can from Torah. We learn every tractate in
Gemara, not only those applicable to the mundane instances in everyday
life. We learn in a straightforward fashion, never delving too deeply into
things. The Rosh Yeshivah and the maggidei shiur teach with simple
but clear logic, so that we understand and we can cover as much Torah
as Hashem wills us.
On Shabbos, Rav Itzele, as the Rosh Yeshivah is known, reads from
the parshah after Shacharis, and expounds on the pesukim with his
insights and explanations. I try to remember them so that after Shabbos
I can write them down in my diary. The diary isn't only for my
chiddushim, Tatte, it's also for the divrei chizuk and hisorrerus I hear

from my teachers here in yeshivah. It is one of those vertlech I would like to share with you.

Last Shabbos, Rav Itzele was discussing how the Torah is a Tree of Life. He said in the name of the holy Rav Chaim that the Torah is our true life support. If we are to imagine ourselves amidst a raging river, about to drown, we would be foolish not to grasp a sturdy branch floating by.

So too, life here in this world is like a storm, roaring and raging, trying to drown us. But Hashem granted us a Tree of Life, something to empower us and help us live. We must cling to it with all our hearts and souls, and it will give us true life, a chiyus in this world.

I felt that this was speaking to me. You see, Tatte, I now know what will help me through the turbulent winds of this cruel world. If I hold onto Torah and internalize it, I will be in the world of ruchani, and I won't feel pulled down by the storm. If I cling to Torah, Hashem will guide me through life, and He will protect me from the elements.

Chaim'ke, too, knows this. I have a feeling that he, too, is cleaving to Torah despite it all. He also knows that that alone will give him life in this world and the Next. He has the power to fight the cruel Russians because he is holding on to Torah for dear life. He knows that if he lets go, chalilah, he'll be pulled under by the raging river and he'll drown. I daven that he remembers this all the time and he never leaves Yiddishkeit, chalilah.

I hope this encourages you, Tatte, because I know it helped me. Baruch Hashem, we have the Torah to guide us in our lives. And baruch Hashem, I am meriting to learn as much of it as I can here in yeshivah.

Please send my love to Mamme and the girls. I miss home, but I am ever so grateful to you for sending me here to learn and live Torah.

Your loving son,

Srulik Segal

16
Galus and Geulah

Siberia, Russia
25 Nissan 5604

Tatte in Himmel, for how long must we be enslaved in this horri-
ble lager? The galus is so, so long and so, so bitter. This past week
was Pesach, and not only did the officers try to make us work
on Yom Tov, but they also wanted us to eat chametz. We scraped
by with water and a few rotten vegetables the cook had thrown
away. We are more malnourished than ever, but to eat chametz
on Pesach? Unthinkable!

I stopped counting how many times we've been beaten throughout
the Chag. For every little tefillah we dared whisper in Andrei's
presence, I was flogged. It seems as if he enjoys whipping me.
My scars are permanent, I fear. When the officers left us alone for
a bit during lunchtime (for the privilege of rest hour was taken
away from us a while back), we spoke about Mitzrayim, and the
nissim Hashem did for us there.

"It feels like Mitzrayim here, with the work and the beatings
every day. Andrei has got to be worse than Pharaoh. I can't last
here any longer," complained Aharon in exasperation.

I was surprised. Aharon complaining?! It isn't like him. His emunah is unshakeable! But then again, the matzav here is so dire; many of us are losing hope.

But we must never lose hope! I admonished myself sternly. We have to remember that Hashem is with us all the time, and the geulah is destined to come, hopefully as soon as possible.

"Strengthen yourself, Aharon," I urged him, speaking with passion and compassion. "I know that this lager may seem like a repeat of Mitzrayim —"

"A repeat!?" cut in Yossel, his eyes two grey pools of misery. "It's much worse! At least in Mitzrayim the Yidden had hope. They had Moshe Rabbeinu. But we, we don't have a Rav. We don't have a navi. We don't know what will be. There is no hope for us here. It's harder to believe here than in Mitzrayim."

"Don't say that!" Moishele's firm answer was swift in coming. He knew we couldn't give up under any circumstances!

Yossel stared at Moishele, and shrank back in fright. Moishele usually wasn't so strongly opinionated. He was soft-spoken, gentle, and loving.

"There is always hope!" Moishele continued with his words full of warmth. "Hashem is with us, even now! He told Moshe Rabbeinu to tell the Yidden, 'Imo Anochi b'tzarah'—I am with you in your sorrow! It didn't only mean in Mitzrayim. Hashem is talking to us here, now. The Yidden are never lost or alone, even here in this dreadful place!"

"And Hashem saved the Yidden with great miracles," I reminded them all, injecting willpower in the forlorn atmosphere. "He sent the makkos to the Egyptians, remember? He made sure that the Yidden didn't suffer more than they had to. He shortened the galus for them because they couldn't hold out any longer. Hashem knows what is going on here. He sees us all the time. He is with us, even during the hard times. We need to believe that He will bring the geulah as soon as possible."

"But it's still so challenging to have faith in Hashem here," objected Cheskel, as a large tear rolled down his sunken cheek. He looked starved. We all did. "We don't see open miracles every day. All we have here is the cruel Russians and the hard work. It doesn't seem like Hashem is with us."

"Of course Hashem is with us, Cheskel!" I replied with conviction, squeezing his hand in comfort. "Don't even think otherwise! Even if we can't see Hashem here, we must believe it, because He is here, right now. It's a time of hester panim, like during the Megillah. We can't see Hashem's nissim openly and clearly, but Hashem is here, with us, making sure we are holding strong. For now, we have to daven to Him to give us strength to stay firm in our Yiddishkeit."

We can't give up, just like that. We must hold on with all our strength! Just like the Yidden in Mitzrayim, we are crying from the depths of Gehinnom in This World. Please, Tatte in Himmel, hear our cries, and give us koach to stay loyal to Your Torah!

Chaim'ke Segal
Age 14

Siberia, Russia
5 Av 5604

Is there any Shabbos when they'll stop trying to make us work? I suppose not. It was hard yesterday, but we wouldn't give up the Shabbos for anything! Every Shabbos, Andrei tests another boy, to see if he'll give in. This time, Andrei picked on Yossel. He whipped him again and again until Yossel could barely breathe. When he noticed that poor Yossel was about to pass out, he gave up, defeated, and cast the boy on the ground, barely alive. I guess he was disappointed that Yossel was so strong to resist him despite the torture.

We helped him to the barracks to rest, because we know that at the infirmary, they'll force him to eat treife food. I gave him some water from my canteen to wet his dry lips. Cheskel ran off somewhere, and a few minutes later emerged with a bowl of grease, to use as a salve for Yossel's wounds. I don't know where he got it from. He always manages this feat. He must have begged it from the officers, from Yuri, probably. It alleviated the pain a bit, baruch Hashem. When Yossel felt a little better, he turned to me with a question.

"Chaim'ke, you tell us that we get s'char for keeping the mitzvos, but where? When? Don't we get paid back in this World and in the Next? Shabbos is supposed to be a taste of Olam Haba. This doesn't seem like Olam Haba. What good is it to be in this lager, under the rule of the reshaim, who oppress us to no end?" he asked plaintively, his faith waning.

"Yossel," I responded resolutely, dabbing the grease carefully on his raw back with extra vigor, "we only gain from holding on to Yiddishkeit. Even if we don't see the outcomes of our deeds now, we must believe with our full hearts that we never lose out from doing mitzvos. 'Tzaddik Hashem b'chol d'rachav.' The Basheffer is just in His ways. We are not able to understand the cheshbonos in Shamayim, but we are assured that only good will come out of this. Don't worry. It can only be good."

Baruch Hashem, this mollified him, and gave comfort to the rest of us, knowing that we aren't resisting the persecution for naught. I reread my previous entries to strengthen myself and answer Yossel. I thank the Basheffer immensely for my diary, for it gives me life and hope.

Chaim'ke Segal
Age 14

17
Shaken But Shtark

Volozhin, Russia
10 Elul 5604

Srulik walked briskly down the street, deep in thought. He was on his way back to *yeshivah* after eating supper with a family in the vicinity. Since there was no communal kitchen in *yeshivah*, the boys were put up in various homes in the town. Every few boys lived with a family in Volozhin, who was paid to provide food and sleeping quarters for the *Bnei Yeshivah*, the *yeshivah* students. This system, which Rav Chaim Volozhiner created, ensured that the students received food every day, even though the *yeshivah* had no funding for meals. It was considered an honor in Volozhin to host a *Ben Yeshivah* in one's home, and at this time, there was not one family that did not house a *yeshivah* student.

Srulik, together with his friend Mordche, had just finished a pleasant meal at their host and they were now headed back to *yeshivah* to continue learning. The mantra of Volozhin was that under no circumstances would there be *bitul Torah*. Torah was learned twenty-four hours a day, no matter what happened. Srulik and Mordche now hurried back to the *yeshivah*, so as not to waste time for learning Torah.

Suddenly, a cry of terror broke the calm atmosphere. Srulik and Mordche watched in horror as a wagon charged down the street, the horse wild. The driver tried in vain to steady the frantic animal, for a young child was standing in middle of the road a few meters ahead, too scared to move out of danger. He was white with fear, immobile.

On an impulse, Srulik dashed in the street, grabbed the boy, and brought him to safety on the side of the road. The lad, suddenly realizing the severity of the situation, burst into tears. Srulik put his arm comfortingly around the trembling boy.

"Are you alright, *yingele*?" Mordche asked soothingly.

The boy nodded shakily.

"What is your name?"

"D-Duvid'l Smit," he stammered between sobs.

Srulik knew the Smits. Duvid'l's brother, Itzik, learned with them.

"Come," he said gently, leading the boy to his home.

Reaching the little house, Duvid'l ran inside.

"M-Mamme!" he cried, burying his face in her apron.

"We found him outside," Mordche explained quietly. "He was nearly run over by a horse."

Mrs. Smit paled, but emotionally thanked the boys. They quickly left and returned to *yeshivah*.

"That was some scare," commented Mordche as they entered the large *Beis Midrash*.

Srulik was unusually taciturn. Mordche noticed that his friend was whiter than a ghost. They sat down in the *Beis Midrash* and opened their *Gemaros*. But no matter how hard they tried, Srulik could not put his mind to the *Gemara* that lay in front of him.

"*Amar Rava…*" Srulik started, but his voice trailed off. His thoughts were miles away.

"*Amar Rava… Hut Rava gezugt* (Rava says)…" he tried again, but he couldn't continue the *sugya*.

"Nu, Srulik, tell me," asked Mordche playfully, "What did Rava say?"

Srulik didn't reply. His mind wasn't in the *Gemara*. He was carried back to Odessa, a few years before. He was so deep in his recollections, that he hadn't processed Mordche's question. Glancing at Srulik in worry, Mordche shut his *sefer* and pulled his friend's arm.

"Let's go."

"Where to?" Srulik asked, as he was brought back to reality with a jolt. "We are supposed to be learning now."

"We aren't accomplishing much, Srulik," Mordche stated logically. "Come for a walk. Maybe that'll clear your head a bit."

Shrugging, Srulik followed his friend. The boys quietly left the *yeshivah*.

"Sit," commanded Mordche, indicating to a spot on the grass a few meters behind the *Yeshivah* building. It was time to have a serious talk with Srulik.

Srulik meekly obeyed. Mordche plopped down next to him.

"What's wrong?" he queried pointedly. "You haven't been concentrating since the incident today. What's bothering you?"

"Nothing," responded Srulik curtly, absentmindedly playing with the grass beside him.

He pinched his lips together, refusing to talk. He trusted his dear friend, but he couldn't bear to disclose his pain to others. Mordche wouldn't understand him. He can't ever know what Srulik was going through.

"If you share your feelings, it'll ease the burden," Mordche remarked sincerely. It hurt him to see Srulik so... so unlike himself.

After a long stretch of silence, Srulik considered his friend's words and opened up.

"You're right. I guess what happened before awakened memories I don't want to remember."

He stopped to take a deep breath. Mordche waited patiently, worrying for his friend.

"He was frozen in shock," continued Srulik. "Duvid'l, I mean. He was too frightened to move. I... I had to save him, because... when I had the opportunity to save another boy who was also so frightened, I didn't. You see, when... when the *chappers* came for us, one of them discovered the cellar we were in. I saw him and ducked behind a barrel, hiding me from his view. But I didn't pull Chaim'ke with me, and he... he was too scared to move. That's why the *chapper* was able to take him and... and not me. It's *my* fault that he was *chapped*. *I* carry the blame for all the pain of my parents, my sisters, and my brother. It all happened because of... because of *me*. I couldn't let it happen again. So I saved little Duvid'l. But... but Chaim'ke's a Cantonist — and it's because of *my* cowardliness!"

Srulik was crying by now, his voice full of remorse. The emotions came gushing out of him, a burst dam of pain and guilt that was hidden in the recesses of his heart. Mordche put his arm on his friend's shoulder, just as Srulik had done to Duvid'l. He sat quietly and waited for Srulik to calm down a bit.

"Srulik," he told the broken boy, "it's *not* your fault."

He paused, allowing the message to sink in. Srulik nodded slowly, his big blue eyes recognizing and accepting Mordche's words.

"We don't blame anyone for anything, because we know and believe that everything is from Hashem," Mordche continued to elaborate. "It's all in His Hands. It was His Will that Chaim'ke was taken, and it is His Will that you are here. Hashem decrees what will happen, and it will happen, no matter what. Hashem wants Chaim'ke to fight for Him in the canton, and He wants you to fight for Him here, in *yeshivah*. He wants us to delve in His Torah and perform His *mitzvos*. We must do what Hashem wants from us now. What we are supposed to do is accept Hashem's decree with love and follow in His Ways. We must learn Torah diligently and *daven* as hard as we can for your brother, our brother. This is our *tafkid* - to place our full trust in Hashem and go in His Ways.

"Believe in Hashem, Srulik. Everything is from Him, and only He can help us through this *galus*. He is with us all the time, guiding us through the Torah."

Srulik sat still; drinking in his friend's *chizuk* like a sponge absorbs water.

"Th-thank y-you," he said gratefully, his words coming out in uneven breaths. "I-I feel a bit better."

"Baruch Hashem," smiled Mordche, relieved that Srulik was returning back to himself.

"Are you ready to learn now?" he questioned gently.

"Yes!" replied his friend bravely, drying his tears. "Maybe we can learn a special *mesechta* and make a *siyum* in Chaim'ke's *z'chus?*" he tentatively suggested.

"Good idea," replied Mordche, still smiling. This was more like the Srulik he knew!

His friend squared his shoulders and stood up. Srulik was prepared to do the Will of his Creator, no matter what courage it would take. He would fight for Hashem in whatever way he can.

If Chaim'ke can be strong enough to fight, he reasoned, *then so can I!*

18
Beatings and Bitachon

Siberia, Russia
20 Kislev 5605

Tatte in Himmel, please empower us! Help us stay strong! Yesterday, they tried forcing us to work on Shabbos. Again. We wouldn't dare! To transgress the holy Shabbos? Never! But Andrei pulled me aside and had a "conversation" with me. It was brief, and to the point.

"You're the leader," he told me bluntly. "The other boys look up to you, and will follow what you do. Set a good example and conform to the behavior of a good Russian solider."

"I can't. I'm a soldier of Hashem, and will never trample His Torah to be a Russian soldier," I replied quietly but strongly. My point was clear. I wouldn't give up the Torah and mitzvos for anything.

He then whipped me with a horse whip. This whip is harsher than his other one, and is used only for corporal punishment. The beatings hurt more than ever. I felt like the Jewish overseers in Mitzrayim, who refused to tell on their brothers, and they were punished for it. Tatte told us about it once. It feels like eons ago, being home with Tatte and Mamme. I'm forgetting some of what they've taught me, unfortunately, in my weak state of mind. Hashem, please preserve the Yiddishkeit in my mind and in my heart! It's the best way I can stay loyal to You!

I began to count the lashes. Every ten lashes, Andrei would pause to see if I changed my mind. I didn't. Then, the torture resumed.

One, two, three...

Seven, eight, nine, ten.

"Well?"

"I'm a Yid. I will not work on Shabbos for any price."

Eleven, twelve, thirteen...

Sixteen, seventeen, eighteen...

Twenty.

"Did you change your mind?"

"No. I am ready to give up my life for Shabbos."

On and on, thirty, forty, and then fifty.

Sixty, sixty one, sixty two...

It hurts so much; I don't know how long I'll last like this. Still, I mustn't give in. I promised! I must keep my promise to the others. I have to stay shtark in Yiddishkeit!

Sixty five, sixty six...

Seventy.

By that time, it hurt too much to reply, but I made it clear that I wouldn't give in. Still, a seed of doubt wormed its way in my already weak fortress of faith.

What am I doing this for? Why am I so stubborn? To die here, in this forsaken wasteland without a future?

I am a Yid. A Yid must sacrifice everything for the Basheffer.

"Ain od milvado." Hashem is the only Creator, and I will not forsake His holy Torah. He created me; shouldn't I do His Will with my full heart? If His Will is that I die in His Name, I'll be glad to do so.

But it's pikuach nefesh. One must do everything they can to save a Jewish life, even if they must transgress the Shabbos.

The conflict was agonizing; it hurt more than the whipping.

They want to baptize me! At a time of shmad, there is NO pikuach nefesh! I must give up my life for my Creator, even for a mitzvah d'rabbanan.

But it's so hard. Do I really have to die for my faith? What good is my faith here and now? I still have a whole life ahead of me!

A life of what? Of gashmiyus? This World is only a passageway to Olam Haba. Tatte always told us that that's the real world. What I do now will affect my portion there, for better or for worse. If I give in, I'll lose my place there, and then what? What will I be worth without Yiddishkeit and the World to Come?

I must hold on until the end! Hashem is with me, and I am shtark enough to pass this test! I am determined to stay Yiddish, even if I die now! I made up my mind.

Eighty, eighty one, eighty two...

Eighty nine, ninety, ninety one...

I thought of Yechiel, who gave up his life for Hashem. I will take his lead, and be ready to die for Yiddishkeit. An invisible force pulled me through and emboldened me to stay steadfast despite the torture.

Ninety six, ninety seven, ninety eight, ninety nine...

The Heavenly Court seemed to be summoning me. The World of Truth was so near. I knew I withstood this nisayon, and I have no regrets.

One hundred.

It was then that I collapsed. I don't remember much after. It all went black, and when I regained consciousness, the others were hovering above me, crying hysterically. Where was I? Moishele said something, trying to shake life into my lifeless form, but I barely heard him. Everything seemed so fuzzy.

"Chaim'ke, are you there? Are you okay?" a voice infiltrated itself into my consciousness. I think it was Cheskel, but I'm not sure.

"Chaim'ke, what happened? What did Andrei do to you?" That was Yehuda. I recognize his plaintive voice.

I tried to get up, but it seemed impossible. I looked about me. Slowly, everything came into focus.

"I'm fine, Baruch Hashem," I whispered hoarsely, using nearly all of my strength to speak. I gazed up at my beloved friends, who are like brothers to me, and tried reassuring them. "I'm pretty much used to the whippings by now."

Baruch Hashem we care about each other and we lift each other's spirits. I don't know what I would do if I were alone here.

"Aharon, let's help him up." That was Shloime talking. He's always so practical.

I was too weak to support myself, so they carried me back to the barracks, where Shloime applied a salve to the welts on my back. Yuri gave it to him as we were stumbling along, I think. Unfortunately, Shloime's an expert at dressing wounds. After all, I get new ones almost every day. I don't think there is a patch of skin on my back that has no scar.

The pain was so great that I could barely move.

But that night, we had a long talk. I forced myself to muster up any koach I had left to try and rejuvenate the others' resolve. I explained my inner conflict with them, stressing the reward that awaited us when we do Hashem's Will.

"Even though they beat us and constantly want to kill us, we must stay strong and cling to the Basheffer! Hashem won't let the goyim succeed if we are loyal to our faith!" I told them with new-found fire. "Haltz zich shtark, tayere kinderlach! (Stay strong, dear children!)"

Tatte said that things said from the heart enter the heart, and it seemed to be true. The boys accepted my words wholeheartedly, Baruch Hashem. I thank the Basheffer for giving me the right words to say and the strength to go on.

Chaim'ke Segal
Age 14

19
Hidden Hope

Odessa, Russia

11 Adar Beis 5605

"Mamme, please may I dress up?" pleaded Perel, continuously tugging her mother's skirts.

She noticed that Mamme didn't look too thrilled with the idea.

"Please?" she added, practically begging. "Please, please?"

"Yes, Mamme," cajoled Blima with a giggle, "May I dress her up *l'kavod* Purim?"

She was enchanted by that very same notion that her mother wasn't so happy with.

"If you'd like," conceded Mamme, smiling back. It had been a while since Blima was so cheerful. This year, she was in the Purim spirit, it seemed, despite her grief. It would do her good to remain glad. "Go down to the cellar and check the chest of old clothes to see what you can find."

Perel jumped up and down in excitement. She insisted on helping Blima find a suitable costume. Blima cheerfully pushed aside a chest and pulled open the trapdoor. She helped Perel descend slowly, making sure not to trip and fall. She lifted her lantern and looked around. Where was the trunk of old clothes? Oh, there, in the corner!

Blima ran to the large trunk and flung open the lid. In it laid garments of all kinds from years and years ago, telling untold stories of the past. As she skimmed through the pile, she was reminded of the little things that made up the happy memories of her childhood. After rummaging for a while, she spotted a little gray vest that would fit Perel.

"Do you want to be a little boy?" she asked her sister.

Perel nodded eagerly.

"Because Srulik's not here," the small girl explained, "I'll be Srulik!"

Laughing, Blima handed her the vest and searched some more. A few minutes later, she found a pair of knickers and a shirt to match. As she pawed through the chest for a cap, she noticed that there was another set of boy's clothes the same size.

Why do we have two of everything? She wondered curiously. She had only one brother, after all. It suddenly hit her. *Chaim'ke.* She had forgotten about her other brother. A cloud of worry dampened her carefree mood. She leaned weakly against the wall, letting the clothes she was holding fall through her fingers.

Where is he now? Is he even alive? Is he still strong in Yiddishkeit? Will he come back? The questions washed over her like a crushing wave.

How can I forget him? she then chastised herself.

"Blima, are you okay?" asked Perel worriedly. Blima was pale. "Are you feeling alright?"

"Yes. I-I'm fine." Blima responded hurriedly. "Let's go upstairs to show Mamme."

Perel gathered her precious "costume" in her arms and clambered up the drop ladder, but Blima wavered.

"I… I'll come soon. I need to be alone for a while," she softly said to her little sister. She wanted to sort out her thoughts and calm her fears in solitude. She closed the box of clothes with a soft thump and sat on it pensively.

Tatte always says that Hashem is with every one of us, especially when it's hard, she told herself reassuringly. *Hashem is with Chaim'ke now, protecting him and giving him strength to carry on. I hope he didn't give up. Tatte says that the only thing we can do for Chaim'ke is to daven. I always daven for Chaim'ke, but he hasn't come back yet.*

She felt a pang as she sought to clear her mind of such morbid thoughts. *There must be a reason, though. Hmm. Mamme says that Hashem does what's best for us, even though it does not seem so. I suppose this is for our best, just the reason is hidden. It's like in the Megillah - the neis of Purim was hidden, but we know that it was all from Hashem. We know that all this is from Hashem; we just have to recognize His nissim that happen every day. I hope Chaim'ke has a freilichen Purim.*

She took a deep breath to calm her emotions, dusted herself off, and headed back up to help Mamme prepare for Purim.

Basheffer, she *davened, please help Chaim'ke! Help him stay loyal to Your Torah! Please bring him back home!*

Siberia, Russia
14 Adar Beis 5605

Purim is supposed to be a happy day. I don't know how happy it is here, but we have to remain as cheerful as we can, so as not to lose heart. Andrei's question actually put a smile on our faces. He asked us why we agreed to work today.

"It's your holiday, isn't it? Are you finally obeying orders?" he asked, confused but relieved.

"No!" I replied, barely controlling my laughter.

He looked so befuddled; it was quite funny to see uncertainty on his face. After all, he was the commander, and he always knew what to do.

"Purim isn't like any other Yom Tov," I explained slowly and clearly. "Today we are allowed to work, and we are happy to do so."

It sounded as if I was talking to a three year old. Shloime suppressed a giggle. Aharon smirked. Andrei realized that we had successfully turned him into a laughingstock. His face red as a ripe tomato, he began screaming at me.

"You-you-you, come here!" he spluttered, his mouth frothing in anger.

He dragged me to the river at the edge of the lager where we draw water from. He proceeded to dunk me into the water, again and again, until I was barely conscious.

"Insolent Zhid! That's what you get for embarrassing a distinguished Russian officer!" He struggled to hold in his temper. "If you do it one more time, you're finished, Zhid'ke!"

He then cast me aside on the bank like a sack of potatoes. I wasn't scared. He can't harm me; only Hashem can decree life or death.

When I recovered somewhat, I went to work. I found the others in low spirits. They seemed to have lost their cheer when Andrei unleashed his fury upon me. Yuri was supervising us, so I asked him if we could sing while we worked. He didn't mind. I didn't think he would. We sang Purim songs, to remind us of the simchah of the day. It gave us life as we sang of emunah, bitachon, nissim, and the geulah. We are so thankful to be alive as Yidden.

Baruch Hashem, we are smiling, something we haven't done in a long while. No Haman can hurt us, for Hashem is with us. He's hiding His Face, but peeking through the cracks and orchestrating events to bring us the redemption. He helps us in every step of the way, supporting us so that we don't falter in our faith in Him.

I owe thanks to the Basheffer, who in His infinite kindness allowed me to live. I don't think I would be able to hold out for so long without His help. I daven that He helps us further through this tzarah, and saves us like He did during Mordechai's time. "Keili, keili lama azavtani?" Please, Hashem, don't leave us alone here! Strengthen us, like you empowered Esther Hamalkah and the Yidden!

Just like Mordechai refused to bow to Haman, we must also refuse to give in to the demands of the Russians. We have to stay strong to the Basheffer. We are not afraid of the goyim, for Hashem will save us from their hands!

A Freilichen (I hope) Purim!

Chaim'ke Segal

Age 15

20
Cheirus of Choice

Siberia, Russia
23 Nisan 5605

It was just Pesach, z'man cheiruseinu—the time of our freedom. Tatte in Himmel, when will it be our z'man cheiruseinu, our personal geulah?

The first two nights of Pesach, we decided to make a Seder - not a real one, of course. Just one to remind us of the nissim of Pesach. We decided that Shloime would lead the Seder, because he is the oldest. We sat in a circle on the floor, with a blanket spread out in the middle for the Seder table. Since we had no matzah or ka'arah to put onto it, we took turns saying the simanim in Yiddish.

"Kadesh," started Shloime. "Ven di tatte kumt aheim fun shul, tit er zich un di vasse kittel un er macht Kiddush - When the father comes home from shul, he puts on his white kittel and makes Kiddush."

He put on his threadbare coat, pretending that it was a kittel.

"Orchatz," continued Aharon, who sat at Shloime's right. Moishele recited Karpas. When it came to Yachatz, it was my turn.

"Yachatz," I sighed heavily. "M'nemt di mittelste matzah, vos heist Levi, un men tzebrecht es in halb - We take the middle matzah, called 'Levi', and we break it in half."

"That's what the reshaim are trying to do," piped up Moishele. "They want to break us, especially Chaim'ke, who is a Levi."

"But they won't succeed!" said Aharon forcefully.

"No," I agreed. "They won't. They can't. We are Yidden, and nothing can change that."

We all seemed relieved by that. Yossel said Maggid, and then stopped. None of us knew Ha Lachma Anya by heart.

"Who will say the Mah Nishtanah?" asked Yehuda in a worried voice when we had reached Mah Nishtanah.

At eleven years old, he knew when he was to act like an adult and when he was allowed to be a child again. Now, he had transformed into a little boy at his father's Seder table.

"You will!" I replied, mustering up a smile. "You are the youngest, and the youngest always recites the Mah Nishtanah."

With his pure voice, Yehuda asked the four kashes. We helped him along a bit, because it's been a while since we've said it at a Seder, and Yehuda forgot some of the words.

Shloime," he said hesitantly when he was done, "I have a fifth kashe. Is that okay?"

"Go ahead," encouraged our makeshift Tatte.

"Why are we celebrating freedom if we aren't free? We are trapped in this lager for so long, and we are certainly not liberated from galus yet. Who knows if we will ever be free? Why should we remember geulah when we are entrenched in galus? What is the point in us remembering Pesach, then?" Yehuda probed, his eyes wide open in all innocence and sadness.

We looked at each other. What were we to say? There was an uncomfortable silence, and then I spoke. Hashem put the right words in my mouth at that minute.

"Yehuda'le, we aren't celebrating physical freedom. We are in galus, and we will only be free when Moshiach comes. But we are free, really free, even now. We are free to choose Hashem-'U'bacharta b'chaim', Hashem tells us. We can choose the life of Torah and Yiddishkeit! We aren't succumbing to their demands! Tell me, why did Hashem take us out of Mitzrayim?"

"To give us the heilige Torah at Har Sinai," Yehuda answered matter-of-factly, wondering where I was headed with this.

"Yes!" I replied emphatically. "That is how we are free! We have the Torah, guiding us and giving us strength. We have the Basheffer, all the time, because He chose us. Do you know what it means, that Hashem took us as His Nation? It means that we are the servants of Hashem, and we are free!

"True freedom isn't physical. It is in the realm of ruchniyus that we are free. We know where we stand, and we do what is right in the eyes of Hashem. We are where we are supposed to be and we are doing what we are supposed to do. When we follow in Hashem's ways, we taste true freedom! That is the kind of cheirus that we have, even today." I reassuringly put my arm around his starved frame. "Do you understand? We are free Yidden, no matter what!"

"Yes, I see now. Thank you, Chaim'ke," he replied in a soft voice. "I... I feel better than I did before."

"And that is the answer to your questions," put in Shloime. "It says further in the Haggadah, 'Avadim hayeinu l'Pharaoh b'Mitzrayim.' We were slaves to Pharaoh in Mitzrayim, but Hashem freed us with great nissim, so that we can serve Him in true cheirus, even in galus! The freedom of being a Yid lasts forever, and if we weren't taken out of Mitzrayim, we would still be slaves there, and we wouldn't be able to keep Hashem's Torah.

"This is what we are commemorating today," he ended with a broad smile, "our true freedom!"

With that, we continued the Seder. When we reached Hallel, we sang and danced for joy, praising and thanking the Basheffer that He wanted us, out of everyone else, to serve Him and be truly free. This spirit carried us throughout the hardships we endured during Pesach. We are forever grateful to our Creator for making us Yidden and giving us the power and will to remain His loyal servants.

Chaim'ke Segal
Age 15

21
Establishing Emunah

Siberia, Russia
Tisha B'Av 5605

Yossel's question saddened me deeply. I nearly cried in front of him. Where did our emunah go? We have to hold onto it as tightly as we can! We mustn't give up hope, chalilah!

"Chaim'ke, what would happen to us if we convert?" Yossel had asked me earlier, tears filling his gray eyes, creating a pool of liquid threatening to spill over. "Really, I feel as if I can't handle the pain anymore. I know that deep down, neither can you. We can't continue living on like this. If you accept baptism, only in name, you can live! What's wrong with that? We're not really becoming Christians!"

Andrei had noticed that we weren't eating today, and he demanded an explanation. I clarified that we are mourning the destruction of the Holy Temple, and we are fasting in commemoration of that event. He then went to tell the priest, and Father Vladek tried to persuade me that I am wrong, chalilah. He insisted we kneel before him and kiss the crucifix that hung around his neck. We stood before him, motionless. We wouldn't ever give up our Yiddishkeit, but we could do nothing to prevent the poison that flowed from his accursed lips. He harassed us until I couldn't keep quiet at the sound of his apikorsus.

My face darkened with anger and disgust, I spat at his feet. I couldn't contradict him outright, for he was officially in charge, but I couldn't tolerate his blasphemy. I am no fool. I am a Yid, and I will never change my status. And I would never allow someone to openly curse the holy Torah and my people.

Outraged by this degradation of the Church, the vicious priest threw me to the floor and whipped me until blood oozed from the welts on my back. I was nearly unconscious, but I wouldn't give in. As always, the others helped me back to our barracks because I was too weak to walk without support. Shloime tried convincing me to drink, but I turned my head.

"You have to drink now, even just a sip!" he cajoled.

"I'm fasting for a reason," I muttered through dry, cracked lips. "I can't forget."

"It's pikuach nefesh," he objected gently.

He was right. I felt as though I would die of dehydration. I took a sip, just to wet my lips and revive my spirit. I hope I will be forgiven for "breaking" my fast, even though it was less than a revi'is of water.

When we finally reached the barracks, I collapsed on the hard ground, exhausted. Yossel kindly rubbed a salve on my wounds, but it hurt. He cried with me every time I groaned in pain. I tried not to. It would dishearten the others. When I felt a little better, Yossel wanted to know why we were refusing baptism. The struggle is daily, sometimes even hourly. It's draining us of our kochos.

"Yossel," I told him, gathering all the strength that I had left, "we are Yidden. We are special. We are the children of Hashem. Our purpose here is to remain a Yid, to be separate as we can from the goyim. If we assimilate and accept their abhorred ways, chalilah, Hashem will punish us. He will send us the goyim to put us into place. Only this way, we will be degraded instead of being on a higher level than them. If we stay Yidden, we won't need the goyim to remind us who we are. We can and we must pull through, for Hashem is with us."

"Perhaps... perhaps we can pretend to be baptized but keep Yiddishkeit secretly," Efroym offered tentatively.

"Yes," agreed Yossel. "Like this, we can survive under better conditions. It feels already like 'bau mayim ad nafesh.'. How much worse can it get? We are choking under their oppression. They'll loosen their grip on us if we act the way they want, but on the inside, we will remain faithful to the Basheffer nonetheless. Hashem will help us."

"But He is only giving us strength if we preserve our identity," countered Aharon strongly, placing his hands firmly on Yossel's thin shoulder in encouragement. "We must remember who we are and hold onto Yiddishkeit as best as we can, no matter what! We promised each other never to leave our faith! We can't give in to their detested religion!

"Do you understand, kinderlach?" he asked, looking at the others piercingly. "It's pikuach nefesh for us to refuse baptism. We must never, chalilah, mix with the goyim! They will just push us away, to separate us. We don't belong with them. We are not like them. Stay strong, kinderlach. Hashem, the Ba'al Harachamim, will give us power to withstand this nisayon."

Tatte in Himmel, we are staying separate from the goyim. We remember who we are. Please remember Your promise to us and help us remain Your holy Am Yisroel!

Chaim'ke Segal
Age 15

22
Don't Despair!

Volozhin, Russia
20 Elul 5605

"*Baruch Hashem!*" exclaimed Mordche in delight. "We've finished this *mesechta*. We have the *z'chus* of making a *siyum!*"

He glanced at his friend, Srulik. Srulik was fingering the pages of his Gemara, staying silent.

"Aren't you glad?" Mordche asked. His best friend was unusually… morose.

"Of course!" responded Srulik, heaving a sigh. "But…"

Understanding his friend's hesitation, Mordche sighed too. This was for Chaim'ke's *z'chus*. Srulik was now hoping for a sudden miracle to bring his brother home. He was unsure if he'd done enough for his twin. What else could he do to help Chaim'ke? He'd learned. He *davens* all the time for Chaim'ke. Nothing exactly changed from when his brother was caught. Where did all his efforts go?

"Let's say the *hadran*," suggested Mordche, at a loss of anything comforting to say.

Srulik nodded dully. When they reached to "*Yehi Ratzon*" after the *hadran*, his mind snapped at attention and focused on the meaning of the *tefillah*.

"*Anu mashkimim v'heim mashkimim*….we wake up and they wake up… we rise early for *divrei* Torah, and they rise early for petty things…"

We rise early for Torah. We have the Torah to show us the way through life. We are Yidden, we are stronger than the goyim, because we get up for Torah, and they waste their time on emptiness of this world.

"*Anu ameilim v'heim ameilim*... we work and they work... we receive *s'char* for our efforts, and they do not receive *s'char* for what they do..."

We work hard and they work hard. We work hard to fulfill the mitzvos. We toil in Torah. We work for it. We live with it. It may be hard, but despite what the goyim want to do with us, we will always hold onto the Torah. Hashem pays us back for all of the sweat and toil we put into our Torah learning and Torah observance.

Srulik smiled at his thoughts, relieved.

We aren't working hard for nothing. Chaim'ke isn't clinging to Torah for nothing. Hashem is with us, and He pays us back for all that we do in His Name. Hashem takes into consideration all that we do for Torah, and He helps us accordingly.

Hashem will provide strength for Chaim'ke to hold onto Yiddishkeit, so that he can receive his s'char for being a true eved Hashem. Even if it's hard, and even if it is taking a long time, Hashem will help Chaim'ke and empower him to hold on. He will return Chaim'ke to us safely, and He will shower us with His many chasadim. Hashem is with us, and there is a cheshbon for everything.

There is hope for the future. We are Yidden, and Yidden never give up hope! Hashem will help us carry on. We will see the result of our efforts in Olam Haba, because Hashem takes into account all that we do for Him and His Torah! Hashem is with us! Baruch Hashem!

"Why are you suddenly so cheerful?" asked Mordche, gazing queerly at his friend. A minute ago, Srulik was so glum. What happened now?

"I'll explain later," replied Srulik, still grinning. "Why don't we start another *mesechta* for Chaim'ke?"

With hope in his heart and a smile on his face, Srulik dedicated himself to learn for his brother, because he knew that his efforts were never in vain.

Siberia, Russia
26 Tishrei 5606

It was Simchas Torah a few days ago. It's supposed to be a day of happiness over the Torah. We were so broken, however, that we couldn't even muster a smile. There is nothing to laugh about here.

"We must be happy today, brothers!" I said, trying to rejuvenate our flagging spirits.

"But how, Chaim'ke? What's happy here? We have no Sefer Torah to dance with!" objected Efroym, heaving a big sigh.

"But we do have the Torah, in here!" I contradicted, pointing to my heart. "We live by it. We live with it. We live in it. We are interconnected with the Torah. No one can take that away from us."

"But it still doesn't make things cheerful here!" he countered dejectedly.

In a way, he seemed to be right. What was there to smile about in this desolate and frozen lager? But I had to prove him wrong, for the others' sakes. If I'm not happy, they'll lose hope, chalilah. I can never let that happen!

I thought for a moment, trying to come up with a valid refutation. With a sudden stroke of hashgacha pratis, I suddenly remembered what R' Mendel had told us about simchah one Rosh Chodesh Adar. He was explaining what it means to be "marbim b'simchah" - to increase simchah.

"Simchah isn't a physical feeling," I replied finally, a small smile playing on my lips. "It is a cryptic atmosphere that we live in. It exists forever. We have an innate simchah in us because we are Yidden! It's enduring, and we always have to put ourselves into that place of simchah. 'Ivdu es Hashem b'simchah' - serve Hashem with joy! It's a mind-frame we must keep."

My smile grew wider as I positioned myself in that very place of simchah I was talking about. The others noticed, and they, too, were grinning. A smile really goes a long way. The atmosphere in the room had changed from one of despair to one of hope. Yehuda hugged himself, clutching his heart, the vessel of simchah.

"Ivdu es Hashem b'simchah!" he sang out, a beaming smile lighting up his face.

"This is how we live as a Yid," I agreed, invigorated with joy. "We are in the place of happiness, true happiness. We have this simchah because we are completely in Hashem's World- the world of Torah and mitzvos. That is how we can be truly happy here."

"Happiness doesn't depend on worldly pleasures," summed up Moishele slowly, as if committing the lesson to memory, "It's the Torah and mitzvos inside of us the make us happy. We are keeping the Torah here to the best of our abilities, and we are going in the path of Hashem."

"This truly gladdens the neshamah," I emphasized. "The essence of the simchah of Klal Yisroel is the fact that we are Yidden! Kinderlach, aren't we lucky? We have the Basheffer! We have the Torah! We have the privilege of being Yidden, the Chosen Nation!" I cried, jumping up.

The simchah in my heart was overflowing, and I couldn't contain myself. Despite the fact that we may get caught for speaking in Yiddish, I started to sing, "Oy vi git tzu zayn a Yid!"

Together, we formed a circle. We danced and sang songs of praise, thanking the Basheffer for making us Yidden, until we had no strength left to dance. We feel much happier now, baruch Hashem, and we are determined to stay b'simchah, even in this dismal and gloomy lager.

With a heart full of hope, I reread a few of my entries, because I knew it would help me live through this. It gladdened me, seeing

all of Hashem's chasadim here. It fortified my belief in the geulah. I know we can pull through, with Hashem's help. Baruch
Hashem, I can revitalize my weary spirits with the diary.

Chaim'ke Segal
Age 15

23
A Loyal Leader

Siberia, Russia
Zos Chanukah 5606

On this day, Tatte once told us, Hashem sends out the din, the judgment, of the year. He waits for us to do teshuvah, from Rosh Hashanah until now, Zos Chanukah, the last day of Chanukah. Last year, like the years before, has been very hard. They have been years of pain and struggle. The fight with the Russians seems endless. My fortitude is ebbing, bit by bit. My emunah is fraying at the edges, I'm afraid. Hashem, please help me preserve what remains of it!

But I can't possibly give up. I have to stay strong. We are just little Yiddishe kinderlach, "Cantonists" they call us, and we are here to become good Russian soldiers. But we are stronger than they think. We don't let cruel Russians succeed, for we are soldiers of Hashem, and we will only stay loyal to Him.

Every morning and evening, we say "Shema Yisroel Hashem Elokeinu Hashem Echad!" The Basheffer is the One and Only, and we will remain loyal to His Torah, no matter what. We won't, we can't give up our Yiddishkeit! We are walking in the path of Mattisyahu the Kohen Gadol, and we are fighting for Hashem. I feel obligated to follow his holy battle cry, for I am a Levi. Segal is short for "s'gan leviyah."

Because I'm the unofficial "Rebbi" and leader here, I was held responsible for the "mutiny" when we refused to work on Shabbos Chanukah, and Andrei whipped me 200 lashes as a punishment. He says I brainwashed the children against the officers, and he threatened that if we don't give in, he's sending me to the army, even though I'm two years too young. The army is even worse than here, we know. Gevalt! We'll need a lot of siyata d'shmaya to stay Yiddish there!

I could scarcely move my limbs after the lashing, and they still forced us to do back-breaking work the next day. For a moment, I thought of giving up, chalilah. It's so hard to stay strong here! But I knew I couldn't do it. I promised the others. If I go back on my promise, what will be with my brothers' faith? It took superhuman effort to convince myself otherwise. That night, I read and reread my previous entries to refresh my flagging spirits and reinforce my emunah and hope.

Despite it all, we won't give in, for everything is a nisayon from our Father in Heaven. Baruch Hashem, I found a broken candle the officers had thrown away. We used the lantern hanging in our barracks to light it for Chanukah licht! On the first night, we lit it with the brachos and extinguished the light after a half hour to preserve the candle, properly performing the mitzvah of hadlakas ner Chanukah. Still, I'm not sure if it's permitted to fulfill the mitzvah with a used candle. So the rest of the nights we lit the wick without the brachos, but we had in mind the mitzvah. Baruch Hashem, we were able to reignite our flame of Yiddishkeit from this little candle! We are determined to do whatever we can to preserve a spark of holiness in this frozen place, physically devoid of Torah and mitzvos. This reminds us to hold onto our Yiddishkeit, and never to give up hope.

Today is a special day, a day of yeshuos and tefillos. I daven with all my heart that our Tatte in Himmel takes us out of this Gehinnom as quickly as possible. And I know that even when I am still crying out to Hashem, the Basheffer sends the yeshuah. Hashem is "Melech ozer umoshiah umagen" — our King Who helps and saves and protects us. Hashem helps us even before we call out to Him and after we daven for a salvation. He has promised to help us all the time. Until a miracle happens, I hope we have the strength to hold on.

Chaim'ke Segal
Age 16

Siberia, Russia
6 Teves 5606

It's Sunday, the goyim's Sabbath. They don't make us work Sunday, although we usually have to make up for what we missed on Shabbos. Today, though, they forgot about the usual work, baruch Hashem.

Still, Andrei wanted me to draw water for his horse, so that the indolent animal doesn't have to walk a few paces to the nearby river to drink its fill. (The horse's laziness is unfathomable. Amongst ourselves, we call him "Golem.")

Well, I obeyed. I had no choice in the matter. When I reached part of the solid river, I saw a boy with a distorted face staring up at me. I wondered who it was, until it hit me. That was me, reflected on the icy water! I was the one with a gaunt face of ugly welts. Andrei had decided that my back was too weak for a beating (which it was), so he mangled my face with his lash these last few Shabbosos, and it hurts when I talk. But I won't give up speaking words of encouragement to my brothers, despite the difficulty involved!

I haven't seen my reflection in so long; I didn't even recognize myself at first. Then again, how can one recognize a malnourished, beaten lad, on the verge of death? As I struggled to draw water from the nearly-frozen river, I pondered over my obstinacy.

Why am I doing this? I'm not healthy now; I'm near collapse. Who knows if I'll live to see tomorrow? What is the point of my akshanus?

I'm a Yid. I can't give in. A Yid is stiff-necked, stubborn for the Basheffer. I must remain firm!

But it gets harder and harder as the years go on.

That's why I must stay unyielding! I've come so far; how can I turn back and become a Russian soldier? I promised never to give up! After all that I fought for these past years, do I want to throw everything away?

Perhaps... perhaps... should I drown myself, ending my nearly impossible struggle here with the Yetzer Hara?

NO!! What am I thinking?! How can I forsake my brothers here? How will they stay strong then? I mustn't desert from the Army of Hashem! It is better I die in battle, and Andrei would kill me, than if I end my life abandoning my post as a loyal Yid!

Am I normal? I berated myself. What's with me? I can't weaken my resolve now!

On my way back to the officer's barracks, I heard humming. Efroym was grooming Andrei's horse (the Golem), and he was singing quietly what sounded like Tehillim.

"What are you singing?" I asked, curious.

"Ani Ma'amin," was his wistful reply.

Efroym was yearning for the geulah. He was certain that it is coming right this minute. I can't give up when it's almost the time for the Ultimate Redemption! Where will I be then? With the goyim, chalilah? His singing reinforced my decision to stay strong.

You see, I told myself, I must fortify my emunah so I won't chalilah fall again.

With that, I began singing along with Efroym, softly, so that the officers don't hear. We are forbidden to pray in Lashon Kodesh, and if they hear us, we are in big trouble.

"Ani ma'amin b'emunah shelaimah b'vias hamoshiach, v'af al pi sheyismameyah, im kol zeh achakeh lo b'chol yom sheyavo — I believe with a full trust in Hashem that Moshiach will come, and even if it seems to take long, I wait for him every day."

It's true. Like Efroym, I trust that the geulah will come now, even if we've been waiting for so long. And you, dear diary, have helped me to hold on to my emunah for so long. I read you every night now, because it gets harder to remember.

Chaim'ke Segal
Age 16

24
Hashem's Children

Siberia, Russia
4 Adar 5606

The Basheffer is so good to us! I cannot thank You enough, Tatte in Himmel, for the kindness You did for us today! We are stranded in this wasteland, in the coldest, emptiest place in Siberia, but our Father has not forsaken us.

We are only a pint-sized group of boys that are rejected by the Russians and forgotten about by our fellow Jews. But we know that we are never alone. Our loving Father cares for us and looks after us, even though everyone else has abandoned us here. We are left here to die, but the Basheffer gives us the strength to live on. Our Tatte in Himmel loves us too much to leave us deserted here, and He helps us stay loyal to His Torah.

Just today, we were given a bowl of gruel with our small ration of bread! We don't receive the "soup" that they used to give us anymore, so we are practically starving. The bit of bread we are allotted is barely more than a k'zayis. It can never give us enough nourishment each day to do the hard work we are forced to do.

But today, the rasha of a rasha Andrei had a bit of rachmanus in his stony heart. Can you believe it, diary? He gave us a bowl of gruel with our bread! It isn't very tasty, but we can't complain. We have something hot to eat, baruch Hashem, to thaw our insides from the bitter cold. We haven't tasted something warm since... since we have been chapped all those years ago! It rejuvenated us, and baruch Hashem, gave us the strength to stay strong in our faith.

I don't know if we'll get more tomorrow. We probably won't. Today, they had rachmanus on us because it was extremely cold. Tomorrow, their pity will run out, and we will have to manage from day to day with a bit of bread again. But today, Hashem showed us His great love for us. He hasn't abandoned us! Baruch Hashem, our emunah was strengthened, too.

Whatever happens tomorrow, we won't give up our Yiddishkeit! They beat us and torture us, in an effort to squeeze Yiddishkeit out of us, chalilah. Notwithstanding the pain, physical and spiritual, we will never give in. We know that it's all for our best, because the Basheffer only does what's good for His children. Even though it's hard, we will never lose faith.

The Basheffer is loyal to us, and cares for us, even in our sorry state. Shouldn't we be loyal to Him and serve Him in the best way we can? And if Hashem sent us these small miracles to show us how He cares, I'm sure that the geulah, the biggest miracle of all, is on its way!

Chaim'ke Segal
Age 16

Siberia, Russia
8 Sivan 5606

Yesterday was Shavuos, the holiday of Matan Torah. Hashem gave us His most precious treasure — His Torah — to live by and to fulfill. But Andrei doesn't care. He knows that we are the Chosen Nation, and he thinks he can take that holy privilege away from us.

He forced Cheskel to stand on two beds, far apart, holding a heavy box of sand above his head. He was not allowed to move until he was ready to accept baptism, which of course, he didn't. He stood there for hours, pleading to Andrei to let him go. Cheskel's woeful tears could melt the stoniest of hearts, but Andrei was an exception, unfortunately. That cold-hearted rasha told him that he can't go until he converts.

After a long while, Cheskel fell off the beds from weakness and exhaustion. The box of sand crashed to the floor, causing an ear-splitting noise. I got scared and ran into the barracks, but Andrei pushed me out. The box cracked open, and sand was spread all over the floor. Then, Cheskel told us, Andrei whipped him for moving without permission. Where is that beast's mercy? He whipped Cheskel until the boy fainted.

That's how we found him later, limp amidst sand and blood. We revived him, and helped him regain a bit of his strength. He looked at us pathetically and burst into tears.

"Chaim'ke," he sobbed, "I can't anymore! What is the point? Why are we different from the goyim? It is so much easier to be a Russian peasant. I know I promised never to give up, but I can't take it anymore! It seems impossible! Please, Chaim'ke, give me chizuk! I'm afraid that if I undergo another torture, I'll give up, chalilah!"

I put my arm around his bony shoulders comfortingly, thinking of what to tell him.

"Cheskel, it's Shavuos today," I told him soothingly. "Hashem chose us today to be His Nation. He gave us the Torah to live by it. We are Yidden, and the Basheffer is always with us. Despite the challenges and hardships, we can pull through. We must, for we are Hashem's Army. We have one mission - to stay loyal to our Tatte in Himmel. Hashem will help us survive this; we just have to daven to Him. We must cling to His Torah, for it is the only thing that gives us life: 'Eitz chaim he lamachazikim ba' — It is a Tree of Life to those who hold onto it! Strengthen yourself, Cheskel. Hashem will help us through this."

He nodded meekly, rubbing his red cheeks vigorously to dry his tears.

"I-I'll try. But please help me, Chaim'ke!"

"Don't worry," I reassured him, hugging him tightly. "Hashem is with us."

"On Shavuos, Hashem promised never to forsake us," added Moishele softly and encouragingly. "We are bound to Hashem, and He won't ever leave us alone here."

Baruch Hashem, we can pass this test, because we have Hashem and the Torah. We are Hashem's holy children, no matter what! "Am Yisroel chai l'olam" — the Jewish People live forever, despite what Andrei thinks!

Chaim'ke Segal
Age 16

25
A New Tomorrow

Odessa, Russia
1 Tishrei 5607

"*Unesaneh tokef kedushas hayom…*" R' Segal sang with trepidation.

As the Rav of the town, he *davened* from the *amud* during the *Yomim Noraim*, leading the *Yidden* of Odessa in prayer for the New Year. The voices of the congregants rose and swelled, entreating to their Creator for a year full of life on this holy day, the day all of Creation passes before the Eternal Judge for inspection.

"*Mi yichyeh umi yamus… who will live and who will die…*"
Will Chaim'ke live through this year? Will he emerge from the canton as a Yid? It's been five years already. Five long, hard years. Can he hold out for so long?

The questions rang in the Rav's ears as he chanted the frightening words. It was Judgment Day. What judgment awaited his son this year?

"*Mi yishakait umi yitaraif… - who will rest in peace and who will be persecuted…*"
Who knows what horrors Chaim'ke is going through? Can he withstand the tortures of the goyim? Is he enduring the pain as a Yid?

It tore the Rav's heart to think that his Chaim'ke was no longer clinging to *Yiddishkeit, chalilah.*
Hashem, please give him the strength this year to face adversity and stay loyal to You!

His voice shook as he resumed the prayer. Choking on the words, the Rav suddenly stopped. He was overcome with emotion, and he couldn't continue.

In an attempt to control his roiling feelings, the Rav buried his face in his hands. He couldn't handle it anymore. All the grief, the angst, the worries, and the desperation of the past years that he'd been holding in suddenly burst forth. Rav Segal wept. He wept for his pain, he wept for his son's pain, and he wept for the pain of *Klal Yisroel.*

The congregation was shocked. Their Rav had never displayed such emotion before. It hurt them to see their Rav crying before his people.

R' Mendel, the *melamed,* quietly walked up to the Rav and touched his arm comfortingly. There was nothing to say. He knew what had triggered such a reaction. He, too, was worried about his son. He, too, feared the unknown fate of his *ben yachid.* Inside, he was also crying, weeping for his own son, the Rav's son, and for all *Yiddishe* sons who were trapped in Siberian cantons.

After a long moment, the Rav caught hold of himself, drew in a ragged breath, and soldiered on as bravely as he could. He knew he mustn't let his congregation lose hope. He had to stay strong for them. He continued to *daven* with conviction and determination.

"*Useshuvah usefillah utzedaka ma'avirin es ro'a hagezeirah!*" he called out in a powerful voice. *But repentance, prayers, and charity can rescind the evil decree!*

Rav Segal knew what had to be done for Chaim'ke - he must do *teshuvah* and return to the *Basheffer.* He must storm the heavens with his *tefillos.* And he must give *tzedakah* in every way that he can, for charity saves a person from death. He was determined to do what he can to bring Chaim'ke home.

Tatte in Himmel, he prayed silently, *in the z'chus of our tefillos here, please save my Chaim'ke from death, physical and spiritual! Please send a yeshuah for all of Klal Yisroel this year! Let it be a sweet year for all of us!*

Siberia, Russia
3 Tishrei 5607

The New Year began - the Yiddishe year. A new page in our books of life has been opened for us, so that we may fill it with good deeds, or chalilah, the opposite. I hope and pray that it'll be a sweet year for all of Klal Yisroel. The sweetness of Hashem's chasadim, have been hidden from us these past few years. Yesterday and two days ago, we davened Unesaneh Tokef. We knew most of the words, and we discussed the meaning of them.

"It's so hard," Moishele let out a pained sigh. "This past year was so difficult. Who knows what lies in store for us this coming year? It will probably get harder. Who knows if we will be able to endure so much torture? What do we do? What will be with us?"

"We have to take each day as it comes," I told him encouragingly. "Don't worry about tomorrow. Tomorrow is not in our hands. It's all up to the Basheffer. But what is dependent on us is today. Will we stay strong today, or will we chalilah give up? Even if we only have strength to pull through today, we can do it! We don't have to worry about tomorrow. Tomorrow Hashem will give us more power to hold on to Yiddishkeit. If we stay strong just for today, Hashem will help us continue to stay strong tomorrow!"

"Yes," added Shloime earnestly. "All we need to do is to try today, and Hashem will help us through the nisayon. Hashem says, 'Pischu li pe'sach k'chudo shel machat va'Ani eftach lachem pischo shel ulam'—Make an opening for Me the size of a needle, and I will open for you an opening the size of a hall! The Basheffer will carry us through if we take that first step and try our hardest to stay loyal to His Torah."

Baruch Hashem, we have today to do what we didn't do yesterday, and we have tomorrow to hope for the future. We draw strength from today to get through tomorrow; for every day is a stepping stone for the next. As we pass each day's nisayon, we climb the ladder of avodas Hashem. We strive to reach perfection in our love and fear of Hashem, and each day brings us closer to our goal. And baruch Hashem, I have you, diary, to help us through today by drawing from the chizuk of yesterday. Hashem is so good to us!

Chaim'ke Segal
Age 16

26
Wandering

Siberia, Russia
29 Cheshvan 5607

Our group, the eight Odessa boys, is being transferred. I don't know where. I don't know why. What I do know is that it'll be another place where we will have to fight for our Yiddishkeit. I hope we are geared up for this. It may be a vicious battle.

Yuri came to tell us that we are being sent somewhere east. I can't figure out why he's so nice to us. After all, we are just a few miserable Zhids. Andrei ordered us into a wagon that was waiting outside. Before I went in, I turned to Yuri.

"I want to thank you for all the kindness you displayed to us for the past few years," I told him meaningfully.

The thanks came from the bottom of my heart. I know that the treatment could have been worse. Yuri always made sure we had what to eat, even when Andrei punished us and refused to give us meals. Yuri always gave us a salve of some sort to heal our wounds whenever we were beaten. Yuri even made sure we had extra blankets in the winters, because we could freeze in the Siberian weather in our thin uniforms. Imagine what it would have been like to have two Andreis instead of one.

"Why did you do it?" I asked, intrigued and mystified. "We are only Cantonists."

"You are Jews, and that's why I cared for you," he informed me plainly. "I grew up in a small village that had mostly Jews. I was an orphan of five years old, without a person in the world to care for me. I tried to fend for myself, but what could I do already? My mother died when I was young, and my drunken father was sentenced to life imprisonment for murder. I had no other relatives to turn to for help.

"But there was someone who noticed my pain. That was the village Rabbi. He took me in and educated me. He cared for me like a father to a son. He trained me to be the town's Shabbos goy, because I wanted to pay him back for his kindness. When I matured, I was drafted. I knew that I may never see 'my' Rabbi again, and I vowed to him that in return for his care, I would be sure to care for other Jews in need. When I was sent to a Cantonist training camp as an officer, I knew this was my chance. This is how I paid back the honored Rabbi of my town. It is the least I can do in gratitude. Now go," he finished, looking furtively behind his shoulder, "before Andrei beats you for tarrying."

With that, we were off to who-knows-where. I relayed to the boys what Yuri had told me. They were awed by his mentchlichkeit.

"Look how that Rav cared for a human being and the kindness came full circle. This goy now cared for us out of gratitude. We never know the outcome of our actions. You see how important it is to make a Kiddush Hashem?" I emphasized. "We have to be like that Rav, and sanctify Hashem's Name wherever we are, however we can. A Yid is a 'light unto the nations' and we must show the goyim what it means to live in Hashem's World. We have to set an example for them in whatever we do. They notice us, and we have to present ourselves as the children of the King of

Kings. We must be mekadesh shem Shamayim however we can, whether by living or by dying as a Jew."

This thought uplifts us, as we roll through the snow drifts to our destination. It's a long way, but at least we are traveling in a covered wagon without shackles on our hands and feet. Baruch Hashem, we aren't trudging through the freezing snow and we don't have to fight with the icy winds. Our means of traveling is, baruch Hashem, much better than it was when we came the previous lager all those years ago. I suppose Hashem wants us to preserve our strength for the upcoming months and years. Hashem should help us!

For now, we will recite the Tefillas Haderech — the prayer for traveling. I made the boys memorize it, for who knows how many more journeys we'll have to make? Hashem should protect us from all harm, physical and spiritual.

Chaim'ke Segal
Age 16

Siberia, Russia
2nd day of Chanukah 5607

Once again, we're traveling from battlefield to battlefield. I hope we have the strength to pull through this nisayon, even if things get harder.

We have been sitting in silence since the morning. For the past few weeks, we've discussed mesiras nefesh, emunah, and hash-kafah. What else is there to say? Our words of chizuk have run dry.

The air hangs heavily, as each of us sit lost in our thoughts. Who knew what tomorrow's struggles will be?

Cheskel suddenly murmured something, breaking the stillness.

"What did you say, Cheskel?" queried Aharon gently, raising his eyebrow.

Cheskel hugged his knees tightly to his chest and pinched his lips together.

"He's scared," piped up Efroym, who was sitting close enough to hear what Cheskel had said.

Shlomo and Aharon exchanged looks. I think they are also afraid, and they don't know what to say to Cheskel.

"And so am I," Efroym added as an afterthought. "What will be? I'm afraid I don't have enough strength to last as a Yid much longer. They'll surely be much worse than Andrei in this new lager!"

I bit my lip. We are all utterly terrified. We don't know what will happen to us. And Tatte once told us that the fear of the unknown is the worst fear one could have, because there is nothing one can do to prepare himself for the future.

"What if we have a crueler commander?" Yossel continued Efroym's train of thought tremulously. "What if we are forced to convert? What if we must undergo worse tortures than the ones we've already endured? What if..."

Yehuda clapped his hands over his ears.

"Herr shoin oif! Stop it already!" he shouted in frustration, nearly in tears. "Where did your bitachon go? Why are we worrying so much? We know that we are in Hashem's Hands, and no one can harm us. We've been living on nissim since we were chapped. We can only survive with bitachon! What happened to us?"

The sudden outburst shocked us, but Yehuda's words rang true.

"Yehuda is right," I asserted softly, hugging Yehuda close to me. "We must trust in Hashem so strongly that there is no need to be afraid, for we know that only Hashem can decree what will happen to us. 'Habboteyach b'Hashem chesed yisovevenu' - he who believes in Hashem is surrounded by chesed. Hashem will protect us in the z'chus of our firm belief in Him. We just need to have faith in Him."

"Yes," agreed Shlomo after a moment of deliberation. "If we put our total trust in Hashem, He will save us from this bitter fate. 'Yeshuas Hashem k'heref ayin' - Hashem can send us salvation in the blink of an eye. We must believe it with our full hearts."

"Hashem is with us," rejoined Moishele in earnest. "The reshaim have no power over us. 'Utzu eitzah visufar, dabru davar v'lo yakum, ki imanu Keil'. They can think of many different ways to destroy us, but Hashem doesn't let them carry out their plans, because He is with us all the time. He protects us from all harm. There is no need to fear, kinderlach. We just have to strengthen our bitachon in Hashem."

"But what can we do to better our situation?" questioned Cheskel, his voice a bit above a whisper.

"We can daven," replied Aharon tenderly. "Tefillah is our only weapon. Come, brothers. Let us entreat Hashem to save us from the harsh gezeirah of the Cantonists. Perhaps in the merit of our bitachon and tefillos, we will be freed from galus."

We started the twentieth kapitel of Tehillim.

"Lamenatzeach mizmor l'Dovid..."

We are pleading before our Creator to have rachmanus on us as we travel from one forsaken lager to another.

"Eileh barechev v'eileh basusim, va'anachnu b'sheim Hashem Elokeinu nazkir — Some with chariots, and some with horses, but we, in the Name of Hashem, our G-d, will call out (Tehillim 20:8).." The Russians have enough torture tactics for forced baptism to fill an entire book, but we have tefillah. "Hakol kol Yaakov — the voice belongs to Yaakov!" We Yidden, the children of Yaakov, are endowed with the gift of prayer. Our tefillos have the power to tear up evil decrees. Our spiritual power of tefillah and bitachon are much stronger than the physical might of the gentiles. We believe that Hashem is the only One Who runs the world, and we have faith that Hashem listens to our tefillos. We place our full trust in Hashem and His miracles that occur daily. The reshaim can never take away our beliefs!

Please Hashem, hear our cries and save us, in the z'chus of our bitachon!

Chaim'ke Segal
Age 17 (I'm seventeen today. Next year I'm bound to be drafted, but I believe in Hashem's nissim!)

27
Tables Turned

Siberia, Russia
19 Teves 5607

Tatte in Himmel, please fortify our emunah in Your Torah! Help us stay loyal to You!

Leibish, or Leon, as he calls himself, is here in this new lager, as the commander, of all things. Hashem Yeracheim!

I recognized him at once from his flaming red hair. Except now, his hair is a sign of his ire to our stubbornness, not of zealousness for our Creator. Gone are his youthful freckles and his joy of life. A grim look of determination is stamped on his face, determination to mold us into proper Russians. Gevalt! He is now a strapping twenty year old man, and not at all like the invincible Leibish that held us together at the beginning.

He became an officer, and he looks just like Andrei and the other reshaim. He acclimated so well into Russian society, that even the seconds-in-command, true Russian brutes, consider him as an equal! What happened to the Leibish we once knew, the one who stayed faithful to the Basheffer? He said that his decision to convert us is unbendable.

His staunchness is the opposite of ours. We, on the other hand, will never change our faith. Hashem, please shield us from his influence! I'm afraid that the others will compare his life to ours and they'll lose hope, chalilah. They can't give in and accept baptism! It's unthinkable! We must work even harder now to stay Yiddish! Who knows what kind of tortures we'll endure under Leibish's rule, just to force us to convert?

How did we meet Leibish? Well, it's a sad story. When we had arrived at the new canton, the officer who brought us, a brawny soldier by the name of Gregory, pushed us into a barrack and left as fast as he could. He wasn't quite interested in his job of transferring us, and he wanted to be done with it as quickly as possible.

Half-frozen, we stumbled in, noticing that there were two boys sitting on the ground, idle. Why they weren't working we didn't know. They were weak in strength but firm in spirit.

After we exchanged introductions, Shmulik, the older one, took one look at us and asked, "Do you know where you are?"

"We are in a lager, are we not?" I answered, confused by his question.

We certainly weren't in a Beis Midrash, although we wished we were. It didn't take a genius to realize that we've traveled from one Gehinnom to another.

"This is the harshest one," explained Gedalya, the other boy, with a bitter laugh. "Welcome to the canton for the worst cases. Here they try to soften up the ones who remained strong during the softening-up process."

"Uh oh," muttered Shloime under his breath. "Chaim'ke, what did we get into?"

"Hashem is with us," I reminded him calmly, masking my worries. "No reason to fear."

"Where is the commander?" questioned Yehuda, throwing a quick glance around him. "Aren't we supposed to work?"

"They are sending us a new commander," interjected Shmulik helpfully. "The old one quit. He was fed up with us because we wouldn't give up our Yiddishkeit for anything!"

We smiled a bit. It seemed as though we were in good company. With Hashem's help, we'll stay strong in Yiddishkeit here!

Suddenly, the door to the barracks swung wide open. We all jumped, frightened. A tall, handsome officer glared at his new charges.

"In formation!" he barked.

We immediately formed a neat row.

"I'm Leon. I will be your new officer here. I expect you to co-operate. If you don't..." his voice trailed off, noticing who stood before him.

He blanched. So did we. It was Leibish! Leibish Rabinovich, R' Mendel's only son! He stared at us, dismayed. We stood there in silence for a long time. The air was thick with tension, and the stillness was deafening.

"Chaim'ke, why?" he finally burst out in Yiddish, directing his gaze at me. "Why are you torturing yourselves? You'll be able to live if you give in to their demands. If you remain obstinate, they'll kill you! Don't you want to live? What's with you, all of you?"

Gedalya's eyes nearly popped out of his head. The barbaric Russian commander was speaking Yiddish?! He and Shmulik couldn't understand what was unfolding.

But the rest of us did. Yehuda buried his face in my uniform, on the verge of tears. Shloime shook his head in disappointment.

"Leibish..." he started to say.

"You are to address me as Sir. Have some courtesy. I'm your commander now," Leibish said roughly, as if to force respect.

He was acting as callous as Andrei, rachmana litz'lan! It hurt my heart to see him like this.   I was always afraid that this would happen, that one of us would assimilate, causing the rest of us to lose heart and give up. I don't want to think of what would happen then! Hashem, please help us stay strong despite Leibish!

"You converted?!?" cried Moishele in horror.

"I had no choice," protested Leibish.

He said these words as though his choice didn't bother him in the least. He seemed proud that he cast off the yoke of Torah. Hashem yishmor! He is like one of the Misyavnim, the Jewish Hellenists of old!

"I would have died from the persecution," he excused himself, as though he was hoping to appease us. "The Torah commands us to protect ourselves from harm. I can't put my life in danger for nothing."

"It isn't for nothing, Leibish!" I exclaimed, finally finding my tongue. "You told us all those years ago that Hashem is the One Who runs the world. He takes care of us, and if He put us in this situation, He wants us to stay strong in our faith and keep the Torah despite our bitter surroundings. Hashem wants us to cling to Him, and He gives us the power and the will to pass this nisayon. You told us that, Leibish! What happened?" My words came out as a breathless accusation.

How could he have done such a thing, something he had resisted when some of us had been ready to give in? How could he be so hypocritical, to convert when he had emboldened us to refuse baptism at all costs? What happened? He's a completely different person now, not like the one we knew. He lost all the Torah he'd taught us, nebach. I feel as if he's a stranger to us. His ideals are very different than what they used to be.

"What happened?" he repeated incredulously.

He couldn't comprehend my opposition to his decision. After all, I went through much of the same tortures, if not worse. I understood how he felt.

"After they separated us," he defended himself, "I suffered so much in the hands of my host. I couldn't take the anguish, the humiliation, the loneliness. So after two painful years, I converted. Don't look at me like that, Chaim'ke! They forced me! They squeezed every ounce of Yiddishkeit out of my being!"

"Leibish, you are still a Yid, no matter what!" I contradicted him, trying to right his obscured hashkafos. "They can't take that away from you! And a Yid can't just leave the Torah. We Yidden are bound to it! You taught us that! If we are meant to keep it, we must hold on to it with our hearts and souls!"

"But must you really die for it?" he protested, anger and confusion fleeting across his face.

It seemed as though the tortures he had endured had made him forget the very basics of Yiddishkeit that were once a part of him. He doesn't even remember what he himself ingrained in our hearts! So much had happened since then, unfortunately.

"Yes!" I replied vehemently, nearly crying for him. "This World is only a passageway to the Next One. The mitzvos we do here will help us gain our portion in Olam Haba. It is a great mitzvah to die al Kiddush Hashem. If Hashem wants us to sanctify His Name here in the lager, we have to; even if it means to die for His sake!"

"Chaim'ke," piped Yehuda in a small voice, finally lifting his tearstained face off my jacket, "it's very hard. I feel that if they beat me once more, I'll die! I'm only twelve years old! I'm still so young. It's the last thing I want to do! I'm scared out of my wits! Hashem would understand if I am mechalel Shabbos once to save my life. Is it worth it, to die before our time, without having a chance to live?"

"Yehuda'le," I sighed, stroking his tormented face, "I know it's hard. Believe me, I know. But we have to hold on with what we have. 'Kavei el Hashem, chazak v'ameitz libecha, v'kavei el Hashem — Hope to Hashem, take courage, be strong of heart, and pray to Hashem again.' Strengthen yourself, Yehuda. Take heart. Think, Hashem helped us so much until now. Look at the chasadim He did for us: - we have clothes on our backs, a bit of food each day, shelter from the weather, willpower to go on, and the Basheffer to help us through this. He provides us with everything we need. The Basheffer is so good to us. How can we turn our backs on Him, chalilah?"

Yehuda accepted my words, but ~~Leon~~ (I can't call him Leon) Leibish did not. His foundation of emunah had weakened and collapsed.

"If you want to be killed, so be it," muttered ~~Leon~~ Leibish, leaving in disgust and defeat. "I'll give you your orders later. I did what I can to protect you. So don't come crying to me for mercy. I'm warning you now."

We looked at each other uneasily. What did he mean by that? He won't, he can't act like Andrei! Surely, he still had some Yiddishe compassion in his heart!

"You don't know what you're in for. I plan on doing what they did to me, to choke Hashem out of you!" he added darkly.

Cheskel let out a little gasp. Was this the Leibish we knew? He was ready to oppress his fellow brethren to forcibly separate us from our faith?

After seeing our obstinacy and hearing my targeted answers to his arguments, he resorted to torture to accomplish his goal — to turn us into loyal Russians, without a trace of our Yiddishe past. He dragged me by my collar to the wall, where a whip was hanging, ready for a beating.

"Do you see that?" he asked severely. "I am ready to use it, if you make things difficult for me."

I said nothing. Seeing the look on his face and the lash on the wall sent a shiver down my spine. It wasn't the beating I was afraid of. I'm used to that already. I'm scared that what happened to Leibish may occur to another one of us, chalilah. No! I can't let it happen! I am stronger than a commander's whip! We are Yidden, and I am determined to preserve our Yiddishkeit!

He realized that I understood, and let go of me. He turned to leave, but paused.

"Chaim'ke," he tossed out sharply, this time in perfect Russian, "you are made of steel."

"No," I replied, with a sad smile. "I'm made of emunah."

Where did his emunah go? Hashem yeracheim! What will be with him?

When ~~Leon~~ Leibish was gone, I let out a krechtz of anguish for his tormented soul. Shmulik looked at me strangely.

"Who is that? Since when do you know officers personally?" he asked, surprised that the new commander was a Yid.

I sighed deeply. "He was my melamed's son."

"Will… will… that happen to us?" Efroym cried, his voice stilted.

This was our worst nightmare: our oldest brother, our teacher, had become the new Andrei.

"Chalilah!" cried Shloime, setting his jaw in determination. "We are stronger than that! We still have our emunah intact, and we won't give into the cruel Russians' demands!"

"We will keep our promise never to give in to the Russians! We must daven that we stay firm here until the end. Only Hashem can help us now. I hope the Basheffer shields us from the Russian influences so we don't give up," I answered, suddenly weary of my battle with Leibish. (I can't let him be "Leon." It would provide a victory for the Yetzer Hara. Who knows where he'll lead us next, chalilah?)

Hashem should assist us in remaining resolute in His faith. I must keep the boys strong, now more than ever. They won't, they can't get influenced by poor Leibish! I hope Leibish will one day indeed do teshuvah.

Meanwhile, all I can do is daven for him, for us, for me. Perhaps if I reread my entries from earlier, where I wrote the emunah that Leibish had instilled in us, I'll remind myself why I am so stubborn, and I'll be able to withstand his pressure.

Chaim'ke Segal
Age 17

28
Victory and Defeat

Siberia, Russia
22 Teves 5607

Yesterday was Shabbos. Leibish works us to the bone every day, but he isn't so mean to us on Shabbos. He knows that we can't be convinced to transgress the holy Shabbos! Still, yesterday he demanded that Efroym fill up his wood box. Efroym was weak from mistreatment, and Leibish thought he'd give up in his frail state. It was especially cold then, and it had started to snow heavily. The weather was blizzard-like, and it was dangerous for anyone, even a healthy person, to be outside. Efroym heroically refused to transgress Shabbos.

"I won't work on Shabbos," he insisted, no matter what Leibish tried to tell him.

Leibish had a queer look on his face. I guess he wanted to diminish Efroym's tenacity, but he couldn't bring himself to whip the boy. He took down the strap that hung on the wall, and raised his hand threateningly. The strap fell to the ground from his loose grasp. His face red with a mix of rage and humiliation, he knelt down and retrieved the strap.

He lifted his hand again, his face torn with indecision and guilt.

He seemed to be forcing himself to whip Efroym. Efroym arched his back, bracing himself for the blows. Nothing happened. Leibish couldn't beat him. I think he didn't want to hurt us, but he wanted to find favor in the eyes of his superiors by beating a few Zhids. He looked at Efroym, looked at me, and then glanced at the strap in his hand. His Yiddishe neshamah won the battle. He hung it back on the wall, and turned to his victim.

"You will go out and chop the wood," he barked, almost embarrassed at himself for his cowardliness. "You will get no meals and you cannot come back to the barracks until the job is completed."

He then pushed Efroym to the door. Obediently, Efroym left the barracks. There is a small window, and we stood by it for a long time, checking up on our dear friend. Efroym was standing outside, amidst the snow that fell thick and fast, stamping his feet to retain circulation. He was muttering, davening to the Basheffer to help him stay strong.

We davened too, hoping and praying that Leibish has rachmanus on us, just like Hashem does. We sang Shabbos nigunim, trying to remember the simchah and kedushah of the day. But our joy was marred every time we glanced out the window. Who knew how long Efroym could last like that, in the subzero temperatures?

By nightfall, the howling winds stopped and we heard the sound of chopping wood. Relieved that Efroym had lived through the day and was able to do menial labor, I encouraged the others to go to sleep. We would need the rest, because as soon as the day breaks, Leibish will put us straight to work. I remained awake, to wait for the arrival of our dear friend.

At about midnight, a frozen and wet Efroym stumbled in. His hands were raw and bleeding, and he was barely able to smile. I helped him dry off and clean up a bit, and then tried to sleep, but Efroym was coughing terribly. The cold had set in his bones, and I gave him my blanket in an attempt to warm him. He's still shivering, and he looks sick. I hope he's alright.

Chaim'ke Segal
Age 17

Siberia, Russia
Rosh Chodesh Shevat 5607

Hashem yishmor! We've lost four boys today.

Efroym had developed a hacking cough and a fever over the week, and yesterday, he could barely lift his head off the floor. Leibish pulled him up and forced him to work, even though the poor boy had no strength.

Last night, the fever had escalated, and he was semiconscious. I ran to his side when I heard him mumbling and crying in his feverish state. He was near death, I realized, but there was nothing I could do. I murmured Tehillim and caressed his hot forehead with my cool hand. He began a coughing fit, struggling to catch his breath. I tried giving him a bit to drink, but he was too weak to swallow. The coughing had sapped him of his strength to live.

About an hour later, he dozed into a peaceful sleep, never to wake again. I recited Shema for him, and the next morning, I reported his death. Leibish just shrugged, and told me to bury Efroym. His face was ashy gray, though. I wondered if he felt guilty.

When the others heard that Efroym died, it disheartened them.

"What's the point of our stubbornness," moaned Yossel, "if we are to die here in this barren wasteland?"

"We are Yidden!" Aharon countered, full of fire. "We are different than the goyim. The Basheffer is with us, and it is for Him we are dying. Efroym may have frozen physically on Shabbos, but his neshamah was united with the Basheffer when he stubbornly stood up for the Torah's values. His z'chus is warming him now in Gan Eden, I'm sure, as he reaps the reward for his mesiras nefesh. We have a purpose here," he insisted.

I was grateful to hear Aharon defend Yiddishkeit so passionately.

"Still, he couldn't save himself from the elements by clinging to Yiddishkeit," argued Shmulik miserably. "If we convert, we will live normally. We won't be forced to stand in the cold like Efroym. We won't freeze to death. We will be able to get out of here, because we will become soldiers and we'll be treated humanely. At least if we assimilate, we have a chance. Like this we can't live!"

"We aren't living for Olam Hazeh!" cried Shloime in desperation. He looked at me, frantic, his eyes conveying that we couldn't lose our brothers now, after we pulled through so many challenges to remain a Yid!

"What good do we have from the pleasures of This World?" he continued vehemently, his coal black eyes shooting sparks. "We are going to inherit a share in the World to Come, and what we do here affects what we will have there! We are not living for ourselves, for we are only mortals. We are living for Hashem, the Creator and the King of Kings."

"He knows it's hard, and He knows what we are going through, but He wants us to withstand this test, because He knows it's best for us," I stated firmly.

I had to fortify their emunah! We can't give in! If some of us convert, what will be with the rest of us?

"We have to believe that it's the best for us, even though we don't see it. We are Yidden, and our tafkid as Yidden is to serve Hashem, through fire and water. If we are to serve Him here by giving up our lives for Him, then that is what we must do!"

"But we have no hope here," complained Gedalya dejectedly. "We can never be Yidden like the rest of the nation. We are stuck here in who-knows-where, and we have nothing Jewish in our vicinity. No one will ever know of our struggles. Even our parents gave up hope on us. They think we are dead anyway, so why should we stay Yiddish? We aren't returning to our old lives of the Yiddishe shtetl. It's impossible for us to be Yidden. We might as well be normal goyim."

I couldn't fathom what he said next. It hurt too much to believe.

"That's it," he made up his mind. "I have had enough of the torture. What are we doing this for? I'm going to be baptized. I'll be much better off in This World, and I don't care what happens in the Next."

When Yehuda heard that brazen statement, he began to cry. I felt like crying, too. Like a Rav is responsible for the welfare of his kehillah, as Tatte's son, I am accountable for the spiritual wellbeing of my brothers. I felt as though it was my fault that Yossel, Gedalya, and Shmulik gave in. I wanted to stop them, but nothing we could say would persuade them.

Yossel advanced towards the door. I jumped ahead of him, blocking the exit with my body.

"Don't, Yossel! You can't! You promised!" I shouted anxiously. I was ready to do anything to prevent them from converting.

"I can and I will," was his annoyed reply. "That promise is impossible to keep."

He shoved me aside and stomped out. Shmulik and Gedalya followed. We heard them tell Leibish about their decision.

"Good," he complimented them. "It's the right choice. I'm proud of you."

I buried my face in my hands. What can we do now? Tatte in

Himmel, help us stay Yidden! We can't lose any more boys! What will be?

"This won't happen to us," Cheskel whispered fiercely, emboldening himself. "We are stronger than that."

"Yes," agreed Aharon resolutely. He turned to me, seeing my pain. "Don't worry, Chaim'ke. Hashem will give us siyata d'shmaya to fight the Yetzer Hara!"

Yossel, Gedalya and Shmulik are now faithful Russians. They are being sent to a different canton for better accommodations and lessons in Christianity. Leibish is glad that they caved in, and he's losing patience with the rest of us.

There are now only six Odessa boys left in the lager. I am working intensely to preserve our emunah, reviewing with the remaining boys the Thirteen Principles of Faith from the Rambam. I reread my previous diary entries each night to remind myself of the tafkid of a Yid. I can't forget! I must remember, so I can strengthen the others, and we won't get lost, chalilah. Please, Tatte in Himmel, help us stay loyal to You! Strengthen us so that we don't fall!

Chaim'ke Segal
Age 17

29
The Basheffer's Soldiers

Siberia, Russia
2 Iyar 5607

Shloime, Moishele, and Aharon are eighteen years old, and they'll be sent to the front any day now. The battlefield's a scary place, physically and spiritually. In the real army, the Russian army, the commanders won't have any patience for our Yiddish-keit. They'll kill us without hesitation if we dare refuse to do their bidding. There is no way we can possibly live as Yidden in the army. Here, at least, we are able to hold onto our faith. Things aren't so bad here, baruch Hashem. I daven that the boys are strong enough to hold on until the end.

I knew they would need chizuk, so I gave them the tefillin, the one that Yankel found all those years ago. We have been using it every day, and Cheskel merited putting on tefillin for the first time on the day of his bar mitzvah. Some of us haven't been so lucky.

"Here," I said, placing the tefillin carefully and lovingly in Aharon's pack. "You hold on to it. Take care of it properly, and put it to good use in the army."

Aharon looked at me as if I had lost my mind.

"We may not be able to!" he protested. "Who knows what will be

if they find us with a pair of tefillin? It's safer here in the lager because at least Leibish won't punish you for using it. You'll accomplish many more mitzvos with it."

"No, you should have it," I insisted stubbornly. "It'll remind you of who you are, even in the Russian army. Just remembering the tefillin will, be'ezras Hashem, give you strength to stay a Yid, despite it all."

He couldn't argue about that. For now, we have each other to draw strength from. But in the army, they might separate us, chalilah. Who knows if the boys will have energy to pull through alone? If they have the tefillin, they'll have a tangible remembrance of their promise to stay Yiddish, and Hashem will surely help them carry on!

We've come so far, if only we can stay steadfast. I am nearly eighteen and next spring I'll be drafted. Gevalt! Is this meant to be our fate? To serve in the Russian army, after holding out for so long? Tatte in Himmel, what will be?

But I know that everything is from Hashem, and it has to be good. There is a Master Plan, even though we are but pieces in the puzzle of life. Hashem truly loves us, more than a father loves his son. Just like it says, "K'racheim av al banim, richam Hashem al yerei'av"—as a father has compassion on his children, Hashem has compassion on those who fear Him.

Hashem knows what we need, and He saves us from all harm. This nisayon was given to us only out of His great love and care for us. He would only give us a nisayon that we can withstand. Even if it seems like darkness, I believe it's for our best. Galus is dark, but the Torah illuminates the night.

I hope the boys will remember that.

Chaim'ke Segal
Age 17

Siberia, Russia
6 Iyar 5607

The drafts were issued. An officer came today to collect those who
are eighteen. A priest came too, to baptize them before entering
the army. I know him; Tatte always spoke about him. He's a mumar, a Yid who converted willingly to Christianity, rachmana
litz'lan. His name is Father Vasyli, and he causes a lot of tzaros
for Klal Yisroel.

He gathered all the children to the river near the barracks. It's
where we usually bathe and draw our water from. Father Vasyli
dragged Shloime forward, and in a forbidding voice, commanded him to convert.

"Never!" was Shloime's adamant reply.

"Do you mean to say that you're ready to be punished in the up-
per worlds for not recognizing the eternal truth of Christianity?"
asked Father Vasyli, irritated that Shloime wasn't obeying his
demand.

"I am a Yid and I will never give that up. I won't be sent to Gehinnom, chalilah. On the contrary, I will be rewarded for holding up the truth of Torah. Nothing you do can change me from
my status as a holy Jewish neshamah!" Shloime stated proudly
and defiantly.

This went on for a while, the priest shouting at Shloime, his frustration escalating, and Shloime calmly answering back that he
wouldn't be baptized for anything.

Suddenly, Father Vasyli lost his temper.

"Look at me in the eye, you insolent boy! Look in my eyes when
I speak to you!" he roared.

It was then when we realized that Shloime had been avoiding
eye contact with the priest the entire time.

"I cannot look at your face," Shloime replied smoothly, staring past the imposing man before him.

"Why?" asked Father Vasyli, barely able to contain his anger.

"It is forbidden to gaze at a rasha," explained Shloime, turning his face away from the priest.

The priest was speechless. Never was there a boy who answered him with such contempt. The Cantonists were usually scared of him, and they gave in to his demand without a battle.

Here, not only was this boy resisting baptism, but he was also impudent and disrespectful to a holy man of cloth! In a fit of rage, he slapped Shloime's cheek in an attempt to turn it towards him. Stung, Shloime kneaded his bruised cheek but gazed at his feet so as not to look at Father Vasyli.

"You-you-you- insolent Zhid!" the priest sputtered. "I'll show you now!"

He turned to Leibish, who stood there, frozen in shock.

"Give me your handgun!" he commanded.

Leibish hesitated, his eyes darting in fear. Without waiting for an answer, the priest grabbed it out of Leibish's holster and held it to Shloime's head.

"Kill me," Shloime said with composure. "I'm only scared of the Basheffer. 'Hashem maoz chayai, mimi efchad?' A man of flesh and blood cannot harm me, unless the Basheffer wills it. I am not afraid of you."

Before he could pull the trigger, Moishele ran up to the priest and tugged the sleeve of his cassock.

"I'm also to be drafted now. I won't either be baptized. Will you shoot me too?" he inquired brazenly.

If there were more boys refusing baptism, the priest won't kill

Shloime, Moishele reasoned, because he'll be fighting a losing battle. He can't force them all to convert at once!

"And what about me?" piped up Aharon, and in long strides, he reached Moishele. "I, too, am eighteen, and I, too, refuse to convert."

Father Vasyli couldn't believe it. Here were three weak and half-starved boys ready to die for their faith rather than convert and live. The other boys will probably react the same way. Moishele's suspicions proved to be correct.

"It is a pity to waste my bullets on a few miserable Zhids," he muttered, handing back the gun to a stupefied Leibish. "The army will cure you of your stubbornness, if the canton didn't."

With that, he left us alone.

"The boys will leave tomorrow," Leibish told us impassively, and we have tonight to say good bye. He sounded as if he was relieved that they were off his hands, but dreading what awaited them in the army.

We were sent to the barracks to sleep without supper. I don't think we've eaten lunch today, either. Every day, we get less food. They starve us and beat us, to weaken us. They don't know that we are a force to be reckoned with.

We are holding tight to each other, for with encouragement, we can withstand the pressure. Our Tatte in Himmel is with us and will protect us from these goyim.

I thank Hashem that the older boys were strong enough today. They are true role models for us. Their chizuk heartened us to stay as strong as we can and remain loyal to our Basheffer, despite the challenges.

Chaim'ke Segal
Age 17

30
Visiting the Past

Siberia, Russia
7 Iyar 5607

Last night was a nightmare. Literally.

This morning, Cheskel told me what happened. I had a frightening dream, about Mamme and Tatte, I think. Cheskel said I was shrieking and crying to no end. It seemed as if I dreamt that someone was after me. He told me that they tried to quiet me, but I wouldn't wake up. My screams woke Leibish, who stormed in and shook me awake.

"Quiet!" he shouted irritably. "If you wake me one more time, you'll be sorry!"

I was scared to open my eyes in front of him. I could almost see his wrath pouring out like lava spewing from a volcano. He had a terrible temper, one that seemed to have developed when he was taken to his host. In Odessa, he was the most soft-spoken and forgiving boy in cheder. He had taught the little ones the alef-beis with warmth and love of Torah. R' Mendel had been so proud of him. I wonder what Rebbi would say now, seeing Leibish like this. I hope he's davening for him.

When Leibish's footsteps were no longer heard, I dared to crack my eyes open.

"W-w-what's going on?" I asked, disoriented.

The others were crowding around me, though I wasn't quite sure why. Why was I on the floor? What happened to me?

"Chaim'ke!" Cheskel cried, hugging me fiercely. "You had a nightmare. What happened?"

"Are you feeling okay? Does anything hurt you?" questioned Moishele, concerned.

I was worried, too. I hardly ever dreamed of home. I was shocked. What had triggered this sudden homesickness after so many years?

I set my jaw in determination. I must remain strong, for the others' sakes. If I am weak, what will be with them? I sat up, hugged my knees to my chest, and drew in a ragged breath.

"I-I-I'm sorry for scaring you." I spoke almost inaudibly, my voice laden with fear. "I'm just so afraid."

"Afraid?" asked Yehuda in disbelief. I suppose he thought that Chaim'ke has no cracks in his perfect veneer of faith.

"Of the army. Of baptism. And... and... and of Father Vasyli," I explained tremulously.

"Father Vasyli?" Shloime questioned disbelievingly. "What's frightening about him? You told us that no one can hurt us. Hashem protects us all the time!"

"No, I'm scared of what happened to him. He's a converted Jew, and he hates Yidden to the nth degree. His... his Yiddish name is Yisroel. Like my twin brother. The differences are striking. I thought to myself, 'What kind of Yisroel do I want to be? Like Srulik, who is a loyal soldier of Hashem, or like Father Vasyli, chas v'shalom, a traitor to our people, to get fame and glory?' It's eating up my insides." I stopped, not sure how I should continue.

"Chaim'ke," put in Moishele gently but firmly, as he laid a hand on my shoulder, "if we are baptized, chalilah, we'll have physical life. But not a happy one. Without Torah and mitzvos, how can one be happy? Look at the priest. His only pleasure is to torture us. He doesn't care if we convert or not. He just wants to oppress us. He knows that our strength lies in the Torah. That's what he wants to take away from us. But no one, not even Andrei, will be able to separate us from our Basheffer. You know that. Hashem loves us too much to leave us in the hands of the goyim."

"Thank you. You're right, Moishele," I asserted, nodding shakily. "He cares for us all the time. The only thing He wants from us is to keep His Torah. That's our goal in this world: - to cling to Hashem no matter what happens. If we do, we'll be protected from all harm, because Hashem is with us. 'Hinei lo yanum v'lo yishan, Shomer Yisroel — the Guardian of Yisroel never sleeps! Hashem is always looking after us. We have to remember that."

"Even in the military barracks," added Aharon quietly, biting his lip.

"Especially there, where they want to destroy us the most," I emphasized.

We sat in silence for a while, thinking. We couldn't sleep after such a night.

"Can we say Tehillim together?" asked Cheskel softly. "We have to daven for Hashem's help, but I don't know many kapitlach by heart. You know the most, Chaim'ke."

I agreed. Cheskel's words rang true. We needed as many prayers as possible to pull us through these terrible times. Verse by verse, we said Tehillim, entreating our Creator to have pity on us here and strengthen us.

About ten perakim later, before sunrise, Leibish came in and roused us.

"Up! In formation!" he barked.

"But it's..." protested Yehuda.

"Shlomo Kofsky, Moshe Kramer, and Aharon Baum, come with me," Leibish said briskly, ignoring Yehuda.

Shloime, Moishele, and Aharon followed him like sheep being led to slaughter. They looked at each other nervously. Who knows what obstacles they were about to face? I can only daven that they stay strong despite it all.

Even though it was before dawn, the officers took Shloime, Moishele, and Aharon to their wagon and left the lager.

"Take heart!" I called after them, choking back my tears. "Remember the promise! Don't forget who you are!"

Hashem should protect them and keep them firm in His faith. There is nothing I can do for them now, except daven.

Chaim'ke Segal
Age 17

Siberia, Russia
10 Tammuz 5607

Father Vasyli engages in a new game these days. After Shloime, Moishele, and Aharon were conscripted into the Russian army, the priest stayed here to convert the rest of us. He's having a hard time with it, though. Now, he insists on debating Yiddishkeit with me. When he decides, which is usually at whim, Leibish drags me to the priest's quarters. In a closed room, we argue about the undeniable truth of Yiddishkeit and the Torah.

It isn't a fun game, and I come to dread it every time, but baruch Hashem I can prove him wrong. Hashem gives me the chachmah and puts the right words in my mouth to be able to dispute the claims of this apikores. I think it's partly because

Tatte and R' Mendel taught me so much and partly because the priest usually doesn't know what he's saying. He argues about the basics, and I calmly repeat what Tatte has etched in my soul - the fundamentals and foundations of our faith.

We don't really discuss details, but he gets very angry at me and beats me many times. Today he whipped me for what he called "embarrassing the Church."

Seeing that I could not last longer under his treatment, he tossed me out of his room like a weightless rag doll.

Cheskel found me sprawled on the floor, doubled over in pain, barely conscious. He helped me back to the barracks, and put a salve on my wounds, but my body still aches everywhere.

Yet the Basheffer is kind enough to help me through this without crying out. If I cry from the torture, Cheskel and Yehuda will hear and they'll lose heart, chalilah. I can't let that happen.

I reread you all the time, dear diary, so I know what to answer the priest and how to encourage the boys.

Hashem should help us withstand this nisayon with hope and emunah.

Chaim'ke Segal
Age 17

31
Lingering Shadows

Odessa, Russia
9 Cheshvan 5608

The night is truly dark in the winter, Rav Segal reflected, as he headed home from *davening ma'ariv.*

As the day deepened into the twilight, his thoughts returned to the shadows of a painful chapter in his life when Chaim'ke was snatched away from them. He valiantly tried to transport his thoughts back in time, when they had been a whole family, all those years ago.

It was a winter Friday night, and he was walking home from Shul with his twin sons.

"The darkness is so gloomy," observed Srulik, his interest piqued. "Why do we need the darkness? What did Hashem create it for?"

"Hashem lets us rest at night, Srulik, so that we rejuvenate and acquire the koach to do His mitzvos during the day," replied Chaim'ke almost immediately, as though the answer was obvious.

Rav Segal smiled. He was used to the twins' endless questions, and he enjoyed enriching their knowledge and hearing what they speculated.

"You are correct, Chaim'ke," he assented. "But there is another answer."

Both boys gazed at him expectantly, eager to hear a new solution.

"We have the darkness at night so that we learn to appreciate the light of day," continued Tatte. "It also reminds us that although it's dark now, the Basheffer will make the sun rise again at dawn."

The twins contemplated their father's words, and the threesome continued to walk in silence.

"Tatte," Chaim'ke suddenly mused with surprising maturity, "I think Hashem is also teaching us a lesson about the galus. Even though we are living during difficult times, we must remember to thank the Basheffer for the good times He granted us prior to the challenges. And Hashem wants to remind us that although we are in the midst of a dark galus, the geulah is on its way!"

"Yes, tzaddik'l, you are right," he had replied, marveling over his son's wisdom that belied his young years.

How correct he was, realized Rav Segal now with a sigh. *If my Chaim'ke was taken so young, the geulah must be near. I hope.*

"R' Yid?" a voice suddenly whispered from the dark, breaking the stillness.

Startled, Rav Segal jumped. The darkness of evening and his distressing memories had drained him considerably. Every small, subtle noise frightened him. He turned to see two Russian soldiers behind him, blending into the grays of dusk.

"*Ver zent ir? Vos vilt etz?* (Who are you? What do you want?)" he asked them, uncharacteristically edgy.

"R' Yid," the taller one tentatively began in Yiddish, "can you lead us to the Rav? We must speak to him."

"Come to my house and *b'ezras* Hashem, I'll be able to help you," he replied graciously, reassured that these soldiers were apparently Yidden.

Realizing that they were talking to the Rav, the young men exchanged relieved glances. They walked on quietly until they reached the Rav's home.

"Well," said Rav Segal, inviting them into his modest dwelling, "what can I do for you?"

"We are Cantonists. We ran away from our commander. Can the Rav help us? We..." the taller boy's voice trailed off.

"Of course!" Rav Segal replied immediately. "What are your names and where are you from?"

"I'm Cheskel Gordon," said the taller one. "And this," he continued, gesturing to his comrade, "is Yehuda Levin. We are from here, from

Odessa, honored Rav. Can we hide here?"

"Blima, give them clothes to change into," the Rav turned and spoke to his older daughter. "You can stay here until we find a way to get you out of Russia," he added. "I'll let your parents know where you are when we find a safe haven for you, be'ezras Hashem."

Blima quietly obeyed her father. Seven-year-old Perel tagged after her.

"What's a C-c-can…?" Perel struggled to pronounce the word their visitors had used to introduce themselves.

"A Cantonist," Blima clarified with a sigh. "They were snatched from the *Yiddishe* villages when they were very young, because the *rasha* Czar Nicholas I decreed that Jewish boys must serve in his terrible army."

"When did this happen?" asked Perel, frightened. She knew of other scary laws from the Russians, but she had never heard of this decree before.

"It happens all the time," replied Blima gloomily. "In every *shtetl*, the *kahal*, the leaders of the community, give over a group of *Yiddishe* boys to the Czar's soldiers. They usually send poor boys and orphans to the cantons. If they refuse to hand over the required amount, the *chappers* come to take the children on their own accord. They conscript the boys on the streets, whoever they can get their hands on. Once, our *kahal* didn't give over the children, so the *chappers* raided Odessa. But after that, the *kahal* fills the quota of boys every month."

"Is that why Srulik is far away in Volozhin? Because he's escaping from the army?" Perel asked her sister.

"Yes, *shayfele*," Blima sighed again, neglecting to mention that Srulik's twin brother had been caught by the *chappers* all those years ago. Perel had been too young when it happened, and didn't remember that she had another brother.

"Those poor boys. They can't keep *Yiddishkeit* in the army, can they?"

"No, they can't," agreed Blima in a quiet voice.

Is Chaim'ke resisting the goyim's demands, even after so long? Who knows where he is now, she wondered wearily.

With a bundle of clothes in their hands, the girls silently returned to the front room, each absorbed in their own thoughts.

"Here, take this for the journey," Mamme was saying, handing the boys a satchel of food. "It should last you until you'll be able to get kosher food."

"Thank you," replied Yehuda sincerely.

"I may be asking for too much," said Cheskel hesitantly, "but would it be possible for us to get a pair of *tefillin*?"

"Certainly!" exclaimed Rav Segal enthusiastically. He removed a *tefillin* bag that was on the shelf above him and handed it to Cheskel. "Use it well!"

Blima paled as she watched her father. She knew that the *tefillin* were waiting for Chaim'ke. It was the only remembrance of her Cantonist brother. By giving it away, she felt as though her father was severing ties with Chaim'ke, *chalilah*. Her heart ached.

But she knew that if these Cantonists would be using the *tefillin*, it would accomplish much more than it had been all these years, sitting idly on the shelf. They would put it into good use, and perform many *mitzvos* with it. She could see from the expressions on their faces that it would give life to these youths, starved of *Yiddishkeit*.

Still, it was hard to accept that Tatte was giving away the *tefillin*. She sighed.

Yehuda stared at the pair with shining, moist eyes. He and Cheskel were overwhelmed with joy. They could now fulfill the *mitzvah* of *tefillin* for the first time in many years!

"Thank you!" Cheskel said with deep emotion, caressing the small velvet bag.

"Now, about escape," the Rav continued. "I have a friend who is sailing to Eretz Yisroel tomorrow. The ship will dock at Yafo Port. From Yafo, you can travel to Yerushalayim, or another *Yiddishe* settlement. Let's go and see if we can sneak you on to the boat. Come."

He led them to the port, where a Russian captain stood smoking, as though he was waiting just for them.

"Peter, my good friend," called Rav Segal, catching the old captain's attention, "you are sailing this ferry to Jaffa Port tomorrow, are you not?" He looked furtively behind him, and whispered, "Can these young men be smuggled onto your ship tonight? I'll pay you handsomely," he continued to whisper as he pulled out a heavy bag of rubles.

"Certainly!" the captain replied quietly yet eagerly, his eyes glittering at the sight of the bulging bag in Rav Segal's hands.

"Thank you," the Rav said gratefully. "Please be sure they reach Palestine safely. G-d bless you."

He then turned to the young men, and pressed a wallet in Cheskel's hands. Cheskel looked up at the Rav, surprised.

"Be well, *kinderlach*. With Hashem's help, my friend here will make sure that you reach your destination. This money is for any expense you'll encounter, or any bribes you'll need to pay. But remember, a Yid does not rely on the help of man. He places his full trust in Hashem. Whatever happens, the *Basheffer* is with you all the time. He'll protect you from all harm."

"That's what Chaim'ke always told us," murmured Yehuda, a faraway look in his eyes.

"Who!?" asked the Rav, unsure if he had heard correctly and unwilling to believe that they might know his son.

"*Chaim'ke.*"

Cheskel nudged his friend to keep quiet, although he expected Yehuda to do quite the opposite.

"Chaim'ke Segal was our 'Rebbi' in the *lager*," continued Yehuda, disregarding Cheskel's hint. "We were a forlorn group of nine children, and the only reason we stayed strong until now was because of Chaim'ke. Chaim'ke helped us through the years that we were in the *lager* together. But then he was..."

"Was what?" interrupted Rav Segal, his mind spinning. The pale moon cast eerie shadows on the ground from the three men, giving the Rav a sense of foreboding.

Cheskel and Yehuda looked at each other, obviously uneasy.

"He is my son. Do you know where my Chaim'ke is? What happened to Chaim'ke?"

There was a sudden stillness in the air. The Rav saw how they hesitated to answer him. That could only mean one thing...

"*Kinderlach*, please tell me, where is my son?" Rav Segal begged them, clutching Cheskel's thin hand.

Cheskel averted his eyes. He couldn't look at the Rav's face. It hurt too much, both for the Rav, and for himself. How can one be so cruel as to tell a father that his son is... no longer among the living?

But someone had to say it. He took a deep breath.

Yehuda turned his face away to hide his tears. The moon, too, hid its face behind a passing cloud, as though veiling the painful truth with obscurity.

"He... he was killed," Cheskel finally muttered. "A few months ago. There were only... only two of us left from our original group of Odessa boys. The... the others either died or converted. When Yehuda and I were being transferred to a new canton, we fled."

Rav Segal stood there, still as unmovable stone. It... it couldn't be true.

"He was *what*?!" the stunned Rav asked again, barely whispering.

Cheskel couldn't bring himself to repeat what he had said. The silence hung above them, laden with pain.

"He... isn't... here," said Yehuda haltingly, drawing in a ragged breath.

Only then did the message sink into the Rav's consciousness. The flood of sorrow nearly drowned him. In an effort to contain his raw pain and emotion, he bit his lip so hard that it began to bleed.

Cheskel wordlessly pulled out a small, leather-bound book from his pack.

"We found this among his things when... when we buried him. Here."

Rav Segal immediately recognized the volume. It was Chaim'ke's diary. He had given it to his son on the twins' tenth birthday. He took it from Cheskel's outstretched hand, trying to absorb this bitter truth.

Chaim'ke was gone from this world. He had only one son now. His Chaim'ke would only return when *Moshiach* comes.

With superhuman effort, Rav Segal tried to regain his composure. *These boys need me,* he reminded himself. *I must remain strong for their sakes. If they see me despair, they'll lose hope, chalilah, and all of my Chaim'ke's efforts in being mechazek them will be in vain. I mustn't let them down! They need someone to raise their spirits and comfort them, to reassure them that all will be well. As the Rav, I am obligated to help them. I cannot give up hope in front of these boys who suffered so much!*

He embraced Yehuda and Cheskel. "Thank you for telling me about my son. And thank you for giving me his diary. I want to offer you words of *chizuk* as you voyage on to Eretz Yisroel."

He knew that they needed to hear encouraging words from him now more than ever. He would have to grieve later. Now he was compelled to hearten them.

Suddenly they heard the captain hiss, "Are you coming? There's an officer nearby, patrolling the area. We have to hide you immediately. It's either now or never!"

Yehuda and Cheskel exchanged a knowing glance. Though Leibish wasn't present with them, he was still making sure they were in safe hands. He'd promised to protect them from afar in Odessa until they left Russia. Leibish was now true to his word.

They turned to go, and after *bentching* them, Rav Segal walked slowly, thinking, absorbing, feeling the pain course through his veins.

My Chaim'ke, my life, is no longer living. The thought played itself over and over in his mind.

The Rav felt as though he was unable to continue. He stumbled to an overturned crate and sat down heavily. The *tza'ar* he had been hiding within his heart for so many years came gushing out. He cried, like he had on Rosh Hashanah.

He was pure, unblemished. He was taken from me… as a sacrifice for all of Klal Yisroel. My Chaim'ke no longer has a chance to… to live in this world. His life was snuffed out… at the beginning of his adulthood. My son, who gave me life, returned to the Ultimate Source of life.

Rav Segal wept until he had no tears left. At long last, he breathed heavily and dried his face.

I have to stay strong, he vowed to himself. *For my family and for me. We have to pull through with emunah, the same emunah that accompanied Chaim'ke in the canton. My Chaim'ke merited dying al Kiddush Hashem, but we must live al Kiddush Hashem. We must carry on Chaim'ke's legacy of faith and determination. I must remain steadfast, and Hashem will help us through this nisayon.*

How would he tell his wife and children this devastating news? They had always been living with the hope of being reunited with Chaim'ke someday… And Srulik… How was he going to be able to tell Srulik about his brother's death? Srulik, his twin, was still so attached to his brother. How would he ever be able to accept this?

Oy, Basheffer, he prayed silently, as he finally headed home, *please guide me! Please place the right words in my mouth so that I can encourage my family properly through these oppressive times!*

32
Brothers' Bond

Volozhin, Russia
2 Teves 5608

"Srulik," Mordche approached his friend, who was immersed in a difficult *sugya*. He tapped the boy on the shoulder, dragging him back to the real world. "Your father is here."

"Here?" Srulik exclaimed, astounded.

Why would Tatte come to the yeshivah on an ordinary day? I hope everything is alright at home, he thought. *Unless... unless Chaim'ke came!*

With soaring hopes, Srulik ran to welcome his father.

"*Shalom aleichem,* Srulik," Tatte greeted him, looking drawn. "I have to speak to you about something very important."

They walked to an empty side room of the *yeshivah.*

"Why? What happened? Is everything okay?" asked Srulik, alarmed. Tatte looked so worn and aged. What had happened?

"Srulik, two Cantonists came to us a few weeks ago. They had escaped from the army, and *b'chasdei Hashem,* they are now on a ship headed for Eretz Yisroel."

Tatte paused for breath, trying to compose himself.

Srulik was quiet, wondering what this had to do with him.

"They... they said they were with Chaim'ke in the *lager.* Your brother stayed strong in *Yiddishkeit,* they told me, through all those years. Never once did he give up. But..."

Tatte then buried his face in his hands.

Srulik realized that his father was trying to hide his tears. Tatte, *crying*?! Something must be really wrong!

"What... happened?" Srulik's voice was nearly inaudible, frightened.

"But the *goyim*... they killed him, Srulik," continued Tatte, struggling to stop the sobs. "Your brother died *al Kiddush Hashem*. You have to... to sit *shivah* for an hour."

"Dead?!" Srulik couldn't believe it. He looked up at his father desperately, as tears began to flow out of the corners of his eyes. "Chaim'ke is... *dead*?! No. It can't be. It can't be! Tell me it isn't true!"

Srulik held his head and cried, *Oy, heilige Basheffer, I know that it's all from You. I know it's for the best. I tried to grow from this nisayon. I did all I can for Chaim'ke's sake. I've davened. I've learned. I've hoped. Where have my tears gone? Where have my prayers gone? Please, Hashem, show me that my efforts were not in vain! Help me through this, as You empowered and strengthened me until now!*

"Yes, it's true. Chaim'ke gave up his life *al Kiddush Hashem*," answered Tatte, putting his arm around his trembling son to comfort him. "The Cantonists gave this to me before they left. It was Chaim'ke's," he continued softly, removing a small book from his pocket and handing it to Srulik.

"Th-th-that's his diary," stammered Srulik, not sure how to respond.

He took it from his father's hand, as a wave of memories engulfed him. He was transported back to his youth, when they were a whole family. It seemed like eons ago, that tranquility.

After a long moment, Srulik looked up at his father.

"Tatte, I-I always thought that... that just like Yitzchak Avinu at the *Akeidah*, Chaim'ke would be saved, even after being trapped for so many years in the army. I thought that like his name, he would be strong enough to live through the horrors of the canton as a Yid. It seems like he was *really* a *korban*, not... not just tied to the *mizbeyach*. He was really slaughtered as a sacrifice. How... how did it happen?"

Tatte silently flipped through the diary until he reached a page with unfamiliar handwriting.

"Read it, *tzaddik'l*," Tatte told him gently, pointing to the last few entries.

Srulik obeyed, his face growing paler as he read. When he could no longer read another word, he just stared at the pages, seeing nothing. Tatte waited patiently for his son's reaction. At last, Srulik couldn't hold it in any more. He dropped the diary and buried his face in his hands, weeping bitterly.

33
Lifelong Legacy

Siberia, Russia
13 Tammuz 5607

Yesterday, Shabbos, Leibish wanted us to work. It seems that after Shloime, Moishele, and Aharon were drafted, Leibish lost the bit of patience that he had. We wouldn't dare obey his command. How can we even think of desecrating the holy Shabbos?

Leibish then became frustrated that we haven't caved into his demands. He ranted and raved about our impudence, but he still couldn't bring himself to beat us, so he ordered his second-in-command, Alex, to whip the ringleader. He was obviously referring to me. I was the one encouraging the boys not to bow to his demands. It hurts me to say this, but I am the one encouraging the others to resist and refuse our dear friend's command. After all, he wants us to transgress our holy Torah, the one he held so dear all those years ago.

Alex whipped me viciously until I was barely conscious, but I bit my lip hard and forced myself not to cry out. When Leibish thought that I wouldn't hold out any longer, he ordered Alex to stop.

When the officers left, Cheskel and Yehuda brought me to a place to rest and recover. I wanted to help their souls heal, but I didn't have enough strength to calm their broken neshamos. Hashem should give me the willpower to get through this and inspire my brothers along with me.

The only way we can get through this is with the tremendous help of Hashem. Without Him, I don't know where we would be. Everything is from Him. We have to remember that. Even though it doesn't seem as though He is with us, Hashem helps us carry on. He is with us all the time, especially when it's hard for us in the lager. He cares for us and sustains us. He gives us the strength to hold on to His Torah. It is for Him that we are fighting.

Hashem is our loving Father, and He guides us on the right path. He shows us the way to live, through the Torah, because He loves us so much. That is why when we were taken, so long ago, we promised each other never to leave Hashem.

We must follow Him, for what He does is good for us, even though we may not see it. We must always remember this.

That is why I am writing it all down. I'm not only writing it here, I'm also inscribing it into my being, committing all this to memory, and etching it in my soul. If it's a part of me, it'll be easier to resist the Russians.

Hashem should help us here stay loyal to Him and act as we should.

Chaim'ke Segal
Age 17

Siberia, Russia
13 Tammuz 5607 (10:45 P.M.)

Dear Chaim'ke,

They killed you today. Leibish had given us only treife meat to eat. We haven't eaten anything since who-knows-when, but we refused. You refused. You stood strong, serving as an example for Yehuda and me. Angry at your brazenness, Leibish pulled out his revolver from his pocket.

"If you don't eat it, I'll shoot you!" he threatened, although trembling visibly.

"Leibish, you are the one who told us that we mustn't defile our holy lips with treife meat, the first time the officers tried to give it to us. Don't you remember? We are Yidden, and we will never sully our pure neshamos with non-kosher food!" you stated firmly, speaking for the three of us.

You once told us that three is a chazakah. Because of that, we are strong enough to withstand this.

"I'll shoot you. I'll kill you!" Leibish cried, sweat pouring down his face.

But he couldn't bring himself to pull the trigger. This was his Rav's son, from his childhood, and he couldn't harm him. This was the same Chaim'ke who stood before him, his head held high. This same Chaim'ke had emerged a victor of the battles in the canton, and had never transgressed the words of the Torah. Leibish, on the other hand, was too weak to fight and had surrendered to the enemy.

He couldn't kill the tzaddik that stood before him, the one whose pure lips have never touched treife meat, no matter what happened to him. Nothing would persuade you to touch something prohibited by the Torah! Leibish knew that you wouldn't be dissuaded from the truth, no matter what happens.

Chaim'ke, no one can weaken your strength of character and determination. No one can destroy your rock-solid faith in the Basheffer. You lived as a Yid, and you were willing to die as one.

Leibish seemed motionless, unsure of what to do. I couldn't just stand by without reacting, so I knocked the gun out of his hands. It clattered to the ground with a loud thud.

Leibish leaned weakly against the wall of the barracks for support. It looked as if his conscience was eating him alive. He wanted to punish you, but he couldn't bring himself to do so. In his heart of hearts, he knew that you were right, and he regretted his conversion. You ignited his pintele Yid, even though for the past few years it was nearly extinguished. He was at a loss of what to do.

The cruel Father Vasyli, however, had been watching the entire time. His ire grew as he watched a brazen Zhid, too strong to break. He was a true heretic, who converted out of hatred towards his own nation. He loathes anything remotely Jewish. And the fact that you had defeated your commander by refusing to eat treife food, fanned the flames.

Father Vasyli picked up the gun, shouting, "This will give you what you deserve, Zhid!"

He pulled the trigger, and aimed at your heart. You fell to the ground and with a cry of "Shema Yisroel" you returned your pure soul to our Maker.

Leibish looked sick, and he quickly left the barracks. He looked so shaken, as if he felt that he indirectly took your life. He looked like he felt guilty of your murder, and that he couldn't face himself. Father Vasyli stormed out right after, cursing and swearing. I thought priests weren't allowed to swear.

I glanced at Yehuda. He was as frightened as I was.

"Come," I said softly, putting my arm around his trembling shoulder, like you did so many times. "We have to bury Chaim'ke."

He nodded miserably, and we buried you near Efroym. Yehuda couldn't stop crying, but what was there to say to comfort him? We returned to the barracks, and we weren't given any bread to eat. We weren't hungry anyway.

It feels like Tisha B'Av now. These pages are soaked with tears, like a sefer Kinnos. We've just lost our leader, our father, our Rebbi.

You left us orphans, Chaim'ke. Who will strengthen us now? Who will calm our fears of the cruel officers, of whippings, of the army? Who will help us keep the promise you made with us so long ago? Who will lead us through this terrible time?

When we buried you, I found this diary in your pocket. Tonight, I read it with Yehuda, and it gave us chizuk. It was as if... as if you were there with us, encouraging us with your warm voice and your firm emunah.

Yehuda just dozed off, but I don't think I can sleep after what happened today. I decided to do what you always did late at night, to write a diary entry. I felt it was only right to write down my thoughts, as you used to. I hope this entry gives us chizuk, as your entries do.

When he sent us to sleep, Leibish told us that he's taking us to a new lager, somewhere near the Black Sea. They hope to reeducate us, and to chalilah undo your "brainwashing.".

Who will help us stay firmly connected to Yiddishkeit now? Chaim'ke, I know that you are in a better place. I know that it's all for the best. But how can we stay loyal to our Tatte in Himmel without our Rebbi to guide us?

We cried bitter tears, for you, for us, for our Torah. Still, we will try to move on. We will try our hardest to remember what you told us and to hold on to our Yiddishkeit.

You always told us that the Basheffer is with us. I daven that He protects us from all harm. And in your z'chus, we won't ever compromise on our Yiddishkeit!

Tearfully,

Cheskel Gordon

Age 15

34
Flight to Freedom

On the Way to Odessa
17 Tammuz 5607
Dear Chaim'ke,

Leibish seems to be in quandary. He hasn't slept the last couple of nights, and it seemed as though something is bothering him. He has bags under his eyes, and he can't stop sighing. He didn't make us work these past few days, because his mind is preoccupied with something.

As we left the forsaken lager, he was trying to be nice, and he let us sit up front with him for the journey southwest. I don't think he would usually do that, even though he didn't portray outright cruelty, like Andrei. Now he is treating us as equals? What does he have up his sleeve? I'm scared to find out.

After we left the lager, Leibish turned to us.

"We are passing Odessa. I can smuggle you into the Jewish Quarter," he whispered, his voice gruff.

The Yiddish sounded rusty on his lips, because he hadn't used it in so long. He always spoke to us in coarse Russian, pretending he didn't understand Yiddish when you encouraged us. The only time he had used Yiddish was when we first met him as our commander.

"T-thank you," I stuttered, startled at this unusual display of kindness. "Why don't you escape with us?"

"I can't," he replied abruptly, looking away.

I didn't ask any questions. Still, Yehuda and I tried countless of times to convince him to join us to freedom. Leibish wouldn't give in.

"I'm not the same as I was," he finally admitted, quite uncomfortably. "I'm an officer, respected and honored by the Russians. I feel like one of them now. And my life is good, why should I leave it? It's not the way my father wanted. I can't face him like this. I'm too embarrassed. Look at what I came to be! I can't return. I just want to close the door on my previous life. I've changed a lot since we were chapped. You know that. I can never go back to being a shtetl boy like I was before. Everything is very different now."

His thoughts came out jumbled, expressing his confusion and doubt. He sounded like Yossel, Gedalya, and Shmulik, and we answered him with the words that you and the others had told them.

"But Leibish, you are never one of them," protested Yehuda, smiling warmly. "We are always Yidden, whatever happens. You still have that beautiful neshamah that Hashem gave you. You just have to come back and cleanse your soul. Hashem always accepts our teshuvah, as far as we've drifted from Him. You can come back! You're as strong as you were then, when we were taken. Now's your chance to escape! We'll help you do teshuvah. Come with us!"

"And Leibish," I added, "you say that you are embarrassed of your father. What about your Father in Heaven? He cares for you and loves you more than any father would. You may be scared to face your physical father, but there is no need to be embarrassed of our Tatte in Himmel. He is waiting for you to welcome you home with open arms, if only you return to Him! You were an onais, you were forced to convert, but now Hashem sent you the chance to come back. Grab the opportunity!"

"I... I can't," Leibish muttered again, though it seemed as if he was thinking about what we said.

Oh, Chaim'ke! What do we do? Are all of our efforts in vain? What will become of Leibish?

I know what you would say. You would tell us to daven, for that is the only thing we can do. You would say to plead before the Basheffer to bring back His Leibish.

So Yehuda and I started saying Tehillim. I didn't know much, and neither did Yehuda, so we repeated the same few kapitlach over and over. Our voices blended in harmony, entreating our Creator for rachmanus and brachah.

Leibish sealed his mouth shut and sunk deep in thought, a distraught look masking his face. But I knew that there was turmoil raging within him. Of what, I'm not so sure. I guess he knew that we were right, although he couldn't bring himself to admit it out loud. After a while, he spoke to me, his voice full of misgivings. "When you reach the Jewish Quarter, don't mention my name. In the worst case, don't tell my father, or anyone for that matter, what happened to me. My father won't be able to cope with it," he instructed me tersely.

"F-fine," I replied, feeling unsettled. I was afraid that he was upset at our discussion. He didn't look too happy after Yehuda and I begged him to do teshuvah. Who are we to give him mussar? He's much older than us, and he's our superior!

"But-but Leibish, don't think that we just wanted to reprove you. We really are grateful to you for what you are doing. May Hashem bless you for this chesed. We will forever be indebted to you for this."

I was really sincere, but Leibish brushed me off with a wave of his hand.

"I'm not such a tzaddik as you make me to be," he mumbled, but he clearly appreciated the effusive thanks. "Go to the back of the wagon. I see some officers in the distance. I don't want to get into trouble."

I don't know his thoughts, but he seems to be uncomfortable with himself. I think he is caught in the Russian trap of honor, and he doesn't know how to get himself out. Chaim'ke, you are closer to the Basheffer. Storm the heavens with your tefillos! Daven for Leibish as hard as you can! He really needs our prayers to save him from the claws of the Russian yetzer hara!

Leibish told us that when we reach Odessa, he'll take us into the Jewish Quarter at night, so we won't be seen and recognized. It's risky, but I know that Hashem is with us, protecting us all the time.

I looked out of the small window in the wagon and noticed that we have passed a river. You told us that we must say Tefillas Haderech only after we pass a body of water, such as a river or stream.

"Yehuda," I said, "let's say Tefillas Haderech. We really need it, now more than ever."

Yehuda nodded vigorously, and we began the prayer that you committed to our memories when we were transferred this past winter. I thought I heard Leibish join in, in a low, hesitant voice, but I don't know for certain. The wheels of the wagon were clacking too loudly for me to be sure.

Hashem, please protect us! "Yehi ratzon milfanecha..."

With a heart full of hope,

Cheskel Gordon

Age 15

Epilogue

Volozhin, Russia
14 Tammuz 5614

Dearest Chaim'ke,

I don't know how to thank you, brother. You helped me in ways unimaginable. You don't know how many times I've read your diary, and it gives me chizuk every time I read it. I have much to learn from you. Your emunah was so strong, it's unfathomable.

When you were taken, I couldn't move on. It was so hard. Tatte and R' Mendel tried to comfort me, to reassure me. But I couldn't stop thinking about you. After you were gone, I was missing a limb. I was missing my heart. Everything reminded me of you, and I couldn't let go. We were so attached to each other, I felt as though I couldn't live my life without you.

When Tatte told me that... that you weren't with us anymore, we spoke about the good times, and he told me about how you pulled through during the hard times. We learned Mishnayos together for an aliyas neshamah for you, although I'm almost sure you are the closest possible to the Kisei Hakavod now.

Tatte also gave me your diary. I read it, and then read it again. You spoke to me through it. You told me, even though you weren't sitting next to me, that everything is from Hashem. Hashem loves us, and takes care of us all the time. And whatever Hashem does has to be for our best, for He is our Tatte, Who loves us more than anything.

I heard it before. Tatte, Mamme, and my rebbeim say it always. But you modeled it to me. You showed me how to stay strong. You helped me in the best way possible. You revived me; I am able to live again.

I am still connected with you, and I didn't forget you. I can never forget you. But I'm, baruch Hashem, able to move on. You transplanted your heart into me, for I had lost mine. I read your diary again and again, drawing chizuk from your words and pride from your deeds. Hashem has blessed me immensely with a brother like you, Chaim'ke.

I got married, baruch Hashem, four years ago, about a year after Tatte came to tell me the news about... about what happened to you. We live in Volozhin, near the yeshivah where I learn. We have a son who is named after you. Little Chaim'ke'l carries on your legacy of devotion and determination. He is only three years old, but his emunah in the Basheffer and simple faith is solid- like yours. I daven that be'ezras Hashem, he'll grow up to be the talmid chacham you always dreamed of being, with his emunah and bitachon in the Basheffer as strong as yours.

I read your promise, Chaim'ke, the one that you made with the other boys, and I want to make a similar promise with you.

I promise, dear brother, to try as hard as I can to uphold what you held dear, what you lived and died for. I promise to work on my emunah so I can believe the way you did, and do Hashem's ratzon all the time. I promise to raise my family to live Torah, breathe it, learn it, the way you did. And I promise to look as hard as I can and search for the chasadim Hashem does for us every day, even what seems like such a little thing.

I want to live as you did, and make the best of every situation, no matter what life throws at me. I ask you to daven for me that I have strength to keep my promise as faithfully as you clung to yours.

And be'ezras Hashem, very soon, the geulah will come and you will return to us. It's just like you told us on that Friday night so long ago. If the galus seems darker than ever, the geulah must be very near, for the darkest hour is always just before the dawn.

I hope I can hold strong wherever life takes me, just like you did. Your mesiras nefesh and firm faith set an example for me how to live as a true Yid in galus. Thank you for helping me realize that our Tatte in Himmel is always there for us, protecting us and caring for us in every situation.

I'm forever indebted to you, dear brother. You are my Chaim'ke, my life.

L'chaim forever,
Srulik Segal
Age 23

Glossary

All words are Hebrew unless otherwise indicated.

Akeidah – sacrificial altar (referring to the Binding of Isaac in the Torah)

Akshanus – stubbornness

Al Kiddush Hashem – to sanctify G-d's Name

Alef-bais – Hebrew alphabet

Aliyas neshamah – the elevation of the soul in Heaven

Am K'shei Oref – stiff-necked nation

Am Yisroel – the Nation of Israel (i.e. the Jewish Nation)

Amud – lectern

Ani Ma'amin – (lit. I believe) the Thirteen Principles of Faith

Apikorsus – heresy

Asarah Harugei Malchus – the Ten Martyrs

Assur – forbidden

Avinu Malkeinu – (lit. our Father our King) a prayer said on the High Holidays

Avodah – work, service (in regard to avodas Hashem)

Avodas Hashem – serving the Creator

B'chasdei Hashem – with the kindness of G-d

Ba'al Harachamim – the Master of Mercifulness

Bachur / bachurim – teenaged youth/s

(Ha)bachur – (the) adult young man, over thirteen

Baruch Hashem – Praised be G-d

Basheffer (Yiddish) – the Creator

Be'ezras Hashem – with the help of G-d

Beis Midrash – study hall

Ben / bnei yeshivah – (lit. son/sons of the yeshivah) yeshivah student/s

Ben yachid – only son

Bentching (Yid.)– blessing (verb)

Bitachon – faith

Bitul Torah – wasting time set aside for learning Torah

Brachos – blessings

Bren (Yid.) – (lit. fire) enthusiasm

Chachmah – wisdom

Chag – holiday

Chalilah – G-d forbid

Chametz – unleavened bread that is not eaten during Pesach

Chapped (Yid.) – caught, kidnapped

Chas v'shalom – G-d forbid!

Chasadim – kind deeds

Chazakah – establishment

Chazal – (abbreviation for *chachameinu zichronam livracha*) our Sages

Cheder / chedarim – school/s

Cheirus – freedom

Chesed – kindness

Cheshbon/chesbonos – plan/s, accounting/s

Chiddushim – (lit. new things) novel insights

Chiyus – a life force

Chizuk– encouragement

Chumash/chumashim – Bible/s

Churban – destruction of the Holy Temple

D'rabbanan – Rabbinical

Davens (Yid.) – prays

Din – judgment

Divrei chizzuk – words of encouragement

Dovid Hamelech – King David

Ehrliche (Yid.) – devout, pious

Emes – truth

Emunah – belief in G-d

Esther Hamalka – Queen Esther

Eved Hashem – servant of G-d

Flaysik (Yid.) – diligently

Freilichen (Yid.) – (adj.) happy

Galus – exile

Gashmiyus – worldliness, physicality

Gehinnom – purgatory, hell

Geloibt iz di Basheffer! (Yid.) – Praised be the Creator!

Gemara/Gemaros – book/s of the Talmud

Geulah (sheleimah) – (complete) redemption

Gevalt! (Yid.) – Oh no!

Gezeirah – decree

Golem – dunce, dummy

Goyim – gentiles

G-tt zul uphitten! (Yid.) – May G-d protect us!

Ha Lachma Anya (Aramaic) – "This is the poor man's bread," passage recited
as part of the Haggadah

Hadassim – myrtle branches

Hadlakas ner Chanukah – lighting the candles of Chanukah

Hadran (Aramaic) – declaration said upon completion of learning a tractate

Haggadah – text recited at the Seder on the first two nights of Passover

Halachah – Jewish Law

Hallel – (lit. praise to G-d) the second to last part of the Seder

Haman – Haman the Agagite, the antagonist in the Book of Esther

Hashem – G-d

Hashem Yeracheim – may G-d have mercy on us

Hashem yishmor – may G-d protect us

Hashgacha pratis – Divine Providence

Hashkafah / hashkafos – ideal/s, belief/s, Torah perspective/s

Heilige (Yid.) – holy

Herr shoin oif! (Yid.) – Stop it already!

Hester Panim – Hashem's Hidden Face

Himmel (Yid.) – Heaven

Hislahavus – enthusiasm

Hisorrerus – inspirational words

Hittelach (Yid.) – caps worn by Jewish youth of old

Hy"d – (abbreviation for *Hashem yikom damo*) May Hashem avenge his blood

K'zayis – size of an olive (small measurement)

Ka'arah – traditional plate at the Seder table

Kadesh – first part of the Seder on Passover night

Kahal, kehillah – Jewish community

Kapitel (Yid.) Tehillim – chapter of Psalms

Kashe/kashes (Yid.) – question/s

Kedushah – holiness

Kever Yisroel – Jewish burial

Kevurah – burial

Kiddush Hashem – sanctification of G-d's Name

Kinder / kinderlach (Yid.) – child/ren

Kisei Hakavod – Heavenly Throne

Kittel (Yid.) – caftan

Kiyum – permanent existence

Klal Yisroel – the Nation of Israel

Koach/kochos – strength/s

Kohen Gadol – High Priest

Kol Nidrei (Aramaic) – "All of the vows…", the first prayer recited at the eve of Yom Kippur

Korban – sacrifice

Krechtz (Yid.) – sigh

L'Dovid Hashem – to David, G-d is my… (the first words in Psalm 27)

L'kavod – in honor of

Lager (Yid.) – work camp (in this case, army training camp)

Lamenatzeach Mizmor l'Dovid – to the Conductor, a song of David (first line in Psalm 20)

Lashon Kodesh – the Holy Tongue (i.e. Biblical Hebrew)

Licht / lechatelech (Yid.) – candles, lights (singular – lechteleh)

Ma'ariv – evening prayers

Ma'avir sedra – to review the weekly Torah reading with the commentary of Onkelos

Machzor – prayer book for Jewish holidays

Maggid – the section of the Seder when the Haggadah is recited and the miracles of the Exodus are discussed

Maggidei shiur – teachers in a Talmudic college (singular - maggid shiur)

Mah Nishtanah – "What is different?" – the beginning of the four questions in the Haggadah that is said by children during the Seder on Passover

Makkah – plague (sometimes used as a term of tza'ar, one's plight)

Makkos – the plagues in Egypt

Mamme (Yid.) – mother

Marbim b'simchah – to increase one's joy

Matan Torah – the Giving of the Torah

Matzav – situation

Mechalel Shabbos – transgress the Shabbos

Mechazek – to encourage

Mechiras Yosef – the Sale of Joseph

Megillah – (lit. scroll) the Book of Esther, traditionally written on a scroll

Mekadesh Shem Shamayim – sanctifying the Name of G-d

Melamed – schoolteacher

Mentchlichkeit (Yid.) – manners, good ethics

Menuchas hanefesh – internal peace, tranquility

Mesechta (Aramaic) – tractate of the Talmud

Mesiras nefesh – self sacrifice

Midrashim – commentaries on the Written Torah

Mishnah, Mishnayos – the Oral Torah

Misyavnim – Hellenistic Jews, those who assimilated with the Greeks during the Second Temple era

Mitzrayim – Egypt

Mitzvah / mitzvos – commandment/s

Mizbeyach – altar

Mordechai – the leader of the Jews in the book of Esther

Moshe Rabbeinu – Moses our Teacher (i.e. Moses from the Bible)

Moshiach – Messiah

Mumar – heretic

Mussaf – prayer service following the Shacharis prayer on the Sabbath and holidays

Mussar – the study of ethics / morals

Navi – a prophet

Nebach (Yid.) – pitiful (an expression of "Poor thing!")

Neilah – final prayer said at the end of the Yom Kippur day

Neshamah – soul (plural – neshamos)

Niftar (male) / nifteres (female) – (verb) passed away, (noun) one who passed away

Nigun / nigunim – song/s, tune/s

Nisayon – trial, challenge

Nissim – miracles (singular – nes)

Oilah (l'Torah) –go up to the Amud and be called up to the Torah during the Torah   reading

Olam Haba – the World to Come

Olam HaEmes – the World of Truth

Onais – one who is forced (to transgress the Torah)

Orchatz – the second part of the Seder

Oy (Yid.) – Oh! (exclamation)

Parshah – weekly Torah reading

Perakim – chapters

Pesach – Passover

Peyos – sidelocks

Pikuach nefesh – life-threatening

Pintele Yid (Yid.) – the inner soul spark of a Jew

Pshetl (Yid.) – Torah speech given by a thirteen year old boy at his bar mitzvah meal

Purim – holiday commemorating the downfall of Haman the Agagite, during the time of Queen Esther

Rabbanim - Rabbis

Rachamei Shamayim – Heavenly mercy

Rachmana litz'lan (Aramaic) – may the Merciful One spare us

Rachmanus – mercy

Rasha / reshaim – villain/s

Ratzon – will, desire

Rebbi / rebbeim – Torah teacher/s

Refuah – cure

Retzuos tefillin – leather straps for phylacteries

Revi'is – measure of a quarter (small liquid measure)

Rosh Hashanah – the first day of the Jewish year

Rosh Yeshivah – dean of a Talmudic school

Ruchniyus – spirituality

S'char – eternal reward

S'gan leviyah – assistant to the priests (referring to the Levites, who assisted the Kohanim, the priests, in the Holy Temple)

Sefer – book

Sefer Kinnos – book of Lamentations recited on the fast day the Ninth of Av

Sefer Tehillim – book of Psalms

Sefer Torah – Torah scroll

Shacharis – morning prayers

Shalom aleichem – Peace unto you (typical greeting)

Shamayim – Heaven

Shavuous – holiday celebrating the Giving of the Torah

Shayfele (Yid.) – lamb, i.e. darling (expression of endearment)

Shema – (lit. Hear!) declaration of faith

Shir Hama'alos – A Song of Ascents (Psalms 120 – 134)

Shivah – mourning period for the death of a loved one (to sit shivah is to mourn a death)

Shmad – a time of spiritual destruction

Shtark (Yid.) – strong

Shteig (Yid.) – to progress in learning

Shtetl (Yid.) – village

Simanim – symbolic actions of the Seder ritual

Simchah – happiness

Simchas Torah – the holiday following Sukkos when the Jews rejoice with the Torah

Siyata d'shmaya (Aramaic) – Heavenly assistance

Siyum – celebration when one finishes learning a chapter or tractate

Sugya (Aramaic) – tractate of *Gemara*

Tafkid – purpose, task

Talmid Chacham – Torah scholar

Talmidim – students

Tatte (Yid.) – father

Tatte in Himmel (Yid.) – Father in Heaven (G-d)

Tefillah / tefillos – prayer/s

Tefillas Haderech – Prayer recited when one travels

Tefillin – Jewish phylacteries worn during morning prayers

Teshuvah – repentance

Tisha B'Av – the Ninth of Av, a fast day commemorating the destruction of the Holy Temple

Torah – the Bible

Treife – non-kosher

Tza'ar – pain, affliction

Tzaddik – righteous person

Tzaddik'l (Yid.) – little pious one (an expression of endearment)

Tzaros – troubles, plights

Tzedekah – charity

Tzitzis – fringes worn on a four-cornered garment

Unesaneh Tokef – a *piyut* (prayer) that is part of the Rosh Hashanah and Yom Kippur liturgy

Vertlech (Yid.) – short and sweet lessons learned from the Torah

Yachatz – fourth part of the Seder

Yehi Ratzon – may it be Your will (i.e. the beginning of Tefillas Haderech or other supplications)

Yerushalayim – Jerusalem

Yeshivah – Talmudic college

Yeshuos – salvations

Yetzer Hara – evil inclination

Yidden (Yid.) – Jews

Yiddish (Yid.) – Jewish (adj.), Judeo-German language (noun)

Yiddishkeit (Yid.) – Judaism

Yingele (Yid.) –little boy

Yira'as Shamayim – fear of Heaven

Yom Hadin – the Day of Judgement, referring to Yom Kippur

Yomim Noraim – the High Holidays

Z'chus –merit

Zhid (Russian) – Jew

Zman Cheiruseinu – the time of our freedom from Egypt (i.e. Passover)

Zos Chanukah – the last day of Hannukah

Glossary of Phrases

Am Yisroel chai l'olam – the Nation of Israel lives on forever (oft-used phrase)

Amar Rava tanu rabbanan (Aramaic) – says Rava, the Rabbis learn… (general reference used in Gemara)

Amar Rava… (Aramaic) Hut Rava gezugt (Yid.) – Rava says... Rava said... (general reference to Gemara)

Ani ma'amin b'emunah sheleimah b'vias hamoshiach v'af al pi sheyismameyah im kol zeh achakeh lo b'chol yom sheyavo – I believe with full faith in Hashem that the Messiah will come, and and even if he tarries, I wait for him every day. (Thirteen Principles of Faith from the Rambam)

Anu mashkimim v'heim mashkimim… anu ameilim v'heim ameilim – we rise early and they rise early… we work and they work (prayer said upon completion of learning a tractate)

Avadim hayinu l'Pharaoh b'Mitzrayim – we used to be slaves to Pharoah in Egypt (Haggadah)

Avinu Malkeinu chaneinu v'aneinu ki ain banu ma'asim. Asei imanu tzedakah v'chesed v'hosheainu – Our Father, our King, have pity on us and answer us because we are unworthy. Perform with us an act of charity and lovingkindness, and save us. (Avinu Malkeinu prayer)

Bau mayim ad nafesh – the waters have reached the soul (Psalms 69:2)

Bereishis bara Elokim – in the beginning, G-d created (Genesis 1:1)

Eichah yashva badad? – Alas, she (Jerusalem) sits alone (Lamentations 1:1)

Eileh barechev v'eileh basusim va'anachnu b'sheim Hashem Elokeinu nazkir – some with chariots and some with horses, but we call out in the Name of Hashem, our G-d (Psalms 20:8)

Ein od milvado – there is no one other than He (G-d) (Deuteronomy 4:35)

Eitz chaim he lamachazikim ba – she (Torah) is a tree of life to those who cling to her (Proverbs 3:18)

Esa einay el heharim meiayin yavo ezri – I raise my eyes to the heavens, from whence comes my help (Psalms 121:1)

Haboteyach b'Hashem chesed yisovevenu – he who trusts in Hashem is surrounded by lovingkindnessses (Psalms 32:10)

Hakol kol Yaakov – the voice is that of Jacob (Genesis 27:22)

Halt zich shtark, tayere kinderlach! (Yid.) – stay strong, dear children!

Hanistaros l'Hashem Elokeinu – that what is hidden belongs to Hashem, our G-d (Deuteronomy 29:28)

Hashem maoz chayai, mimi efchad? – Hashem is my life's strength; whom should I fear? (Psalms 27:2)

Hinei lo yanum v'lo yishan Shomer Yisroel – Behold, the Guardian of Israel neither sleeps nor slumbers (Psalms 121:4)

Imo Anochi b'tzarah – I am with him (the Jews) in his plight (Psalms 91:15)

Ivdu es Hashem b'simchah – serve Hashem with joy (Psalms 100:2)

K'racheim av al banim, richam Hashem al yerei'av – like a father has mercy on his son, Hashem has mercy on those who fear Him (Psalms 103:13)

Kadesh – ven di tatte kumt aheim fun shul, tit er zich un di vasse kittel un er macht Kiddush (Yid.) – Kadesh – when the father comes home from synagogue, he puts on his white caftan and recites Kiddush (the traditional blessing on wine).

Kavei el Hashem, chazak v'ameitz libecha, v'kavei el Hashem – hope to G-d, strengthen yourself and He will give you courage, and hope to G-d (Psalms 27:14)

Keili Keili lamah azavtani? – My G-d, my G-d, why have You abandoned me? (Psalms 22:2)

Ki avi v'imi azavuni vaHashem ya'asfeini – though my father and mother abandoned me, G-d will gather me in (Psalms 27:10)

Lamah yomru hagoyim – Why should the gentiles say... (Psalms 115:2)

Lamenatzeach Mizmor l'Dovid – to the Conductor, a song for David (Psalms 20:1)

Ma Hashem shoel mimcha – what G-d asks from you (Deuteronomy 10:12)

Melech ozer umoshiah umagen – the King Who helps, and saves, and protects (Shemoneh Esrei)

Mi yichyeh umi yamus – who will live and who die (Unesaneh Tokef prayer)

Mi yishakait umi yitaraif – who will rest in peace and who will be persecuted (Unesaneh Tokef prayer)

Mimama'akim kirasicha Hashem – from the depths I call to You, Hashem (Psalms 130:1)

Oy vi git tzu zayn a Yid! (*Yid.*) – Oh, how good it is to be a Jew! (popular Jewish song)

Pischu Li pesach k'chudo shel machat v'Ani eftach lachem pischu shel ulam – make an opening for Me the size of a needle's eye, and I will open for you an opening the size of a hall (Midrash on Song of Songs 5:2)

Shema Yisroel Hashem Elokeinu Hashem echad – Hear, O Israel, Hashem is our G-d, Hashem is One (Deuteronomy 6:4)

Shivisi Hashem linegdi samid – I place Hashem before me always (Psalms 16:8)

Tzaddik Hashem b'chol d'rachav – Hashem is righteous in all His ways (Psalms 145:17)

U'bacharta b'chaim – and you shall choose life (Deutoronomy 30:19)

Unesaneh tokef kedushas hayom – let us recount the holiness of the day (Unesaneh Tokef prayer)

Useshuvah usefillah utzedaka ma'avirin es ro'a hagezeirah – but repentence, prayer, and charity rescind the evil decree (Unesaneh Tokef prayer)

Utzu eitzah visufar dabru davar v'lo yakum, ki imanu Keil – plan a consipiracy, and it will be destroyed, speak your thoughts and it won't stand, for G-d is with us (Isaiah 8:10)

Ver zent ir? Vos vilt etz? (*Yid.*) – who are you? What do you want?

Yachatz – m'nemt di mittelste matzah, vos heist Levi, un men tzebrecht es in halb (*Yid.*) – Yachatz, we take the middle matzah, which is called "Levi", and we break it in half

Yeshuas Hashem k'heref ayin – the salvation of G-d comes in the blink of an eye (oft-used phrase)